The Judge

The Rotorua Crime Series, Volume 3

Andrew Gilbert

Published by Andrew Gilbert, 2024.

Preface & Warning

I have the utmost respect for the Police and the work they do under the most trying circumstances throughout NZ and I really should emphasise that any similarity to any person living or dead, in this novel, is a sheer coincidence.

Further I should add that I have based this story in Rotorua as it is a town I know well. The story could be based in any town or city around New Zealand and I would go to great lengths to emphasize that comment.

Copying and using

Table of Contents

Chapter 1

T**uesday**

He called himself the Judge.

He had studied the good book extensively and he considered himself one of the providers of morals in a society that was going to the dogs. He had selected the next girl for correction, and he was studying her movements, extensively.

He had been following her on and off for a few days and he was ready to show her the error of her ways. She had just got back from the Pub having had a few drinks and she was already showing signs that she was the worst for wear. She was a typical example of what was wrong with today's youth.

He followed her to her home in Goldie Street and firstly made sure she was going home alone. She often picked up a guy from the pub but tonight she was alone and made her way unsteadily home. There were always guys who would come home with her for a free night of sex and that in itself was enough of a trigger for the Judge.

He followed her as she went up her front path and waited in the dark while she fumbled for her key to the front door. He had to be fairly good with his timing but this girls brain was addled with alcohol so his job would be easy tonight. Once she managed to fumble her key into the lock, he knew he would have a few seconds. Once she pushed her front door open she was easy to overpower her as she managed to get the front door open, and he and the girl were inside. She was surprisingly agile for a girl with an alcohol fueled fuzziness, but he had her under his control and he was himself fueled by adrenaline as he easily overpowered her and pushed her into a chair. Within a few seconds she was muzzled with duct tape and her hands were tied with the same device. Now he could relax and tell her the error of her ways.

By sign language he conveyed to her that he would remove the duct tape from her mouth if she promised not to scream. Gently he removed the tape and she started to demand things such as who he was and why she had been selected.

The Judge hushed her quietly. When she was silent again the judge told her why she had been targeted. He pointed to her breasts and told her she was dressing far too provocatively. Did she not know that the men in the pub were ogling her and if she wasn't so drunk, she would have had any man in the place.

The girl by now had bitten back some of her sheer anger and was replying to the judge that it was the twenty-first century, and she could dress how the hell she pleased. It was not going well for the girl. The Judge had been in two minds as to whether the girl warranted a warning to mend her ways or whether the ultimate deterrent was needed. It was looking as if he would be the one to make the girl meet her maker if she didn't behave more appropriately. The final straw was when she took the lord's name in vain as she asked him if he was some type of Jesus freak that got his rocks off torturing girls like her.

He killed her. Quickly and efficiently, but he killed her. He took his scarf off and strangled her. Quietly he let himself out of the front door and after checking no one was around he made his way a couple of streets over and got into this car and went home. He almost felt sad as he drove home, but this type of girl was one of the main causes that society was going to hell in a handbasket, and he was at least prepared to stand up and do something about it.

Well the day had finally arrived. We were due to set up in our new office today. The DI and the Sarge were sorry to be leaving their old home. Truth be told, I was also a little sad. We had gone over at dawn for the Blessing and the Waiata and the ritual of having a bite to eat. The Boss had gone overboard with the catering, but it was a part of his budget so none of us cared, and the Squaddies had access to the extra food, so they were not complaining either.

At the completion of the food we had all gone home for another hour in bed. I reckon the CI thought we should have been eager to move in, but we all had mixed feelings.

I have to say I had some fond feelings for the new office. I'm not big into the whole Māori thing but the front had been covered with a design based on Māori folklore and it really looked fantastic. In fact the whole building had been purposely designed as a Police Station. It took up a lot more space than the previous one did, that was built in the 1960's I reckon, and it looked pretty poor and very tatty. As an identity for the Police in Rotorua it was a very poor advert! The New one was custom built as a cop shop. As you walked in the door the Squaddies and the Beat cops had a huge room probably over 1000 square feet, whatever that is in metric. We now had the room on the right hand side. We had our own desk that the Sarge looked after, and we must have had 1000 square feet or even more. I might even say that we may have had close to 2000 square feet. The Boss's office was first on the right, then mine, then the various DCs down to the end and back up to the left. In the middle was a decent sized space for a meeting if we needed it

It was a totally new office for us. Someone had made sure the Boss's office was nowhere near as big as the Big Boss upstairs and we all had our own cubicle to work in. Even I, as the DS, had to work in a cubicle. If I needed the Boss's office, it was available to me, but it was not something that I should be overly quick to appropriate. If push came to a shove, I could always use the Interview rooms with their one way glass.

The Boss had a wee row with the Big Boss as his office did not have walls that went all the way up to the ceiling. I don't think it was a power thing but my Boss wanted a little privacy if he was having a quiet word with someone. The Boss and the Big Boss had one of their semi regular blowups about the issue and my Boss got his way. He now had an office where the walls went to the ceiling. They do have a semiregular bust up and it allows them to vent all of their accumulated feelings. At least that is what the Boss says.

We were moving our gear over to the new office via the use of a Police Van to do the lifting and we were blessed with decent weather for a change. It had been a bit mixed over the previous few days but today the sun was shining on our toil. We had all met with the new boys the CI had promised us. Mike Jackson, and Alan Kirk were the local lads and a lad from Hamilton had asked for a transfer and ended up with our office. Oh and his name was Derek Hildebrandt. He seemed like a nice lad. He was well missed by his mates in the Hamilton nick so that was a good sign for us.

It was expected that we would be up and operating as a unit within a few days and we would be operating under the Big Boss's proposed scheme within a week of setting up. It would have been about 9.30 when we got the call about a possible murder in Goldie St. The Boss was busy setting his office up, so he told myself and Mike Jackson to go up and check it out. I should add that the Boss's new office was only about half the size of his previous office and things were not going well as the Boss tried to unpack all of his gear.

Driving up to Goldie St was the first time I had worked with Mike. He seemed keen to do well. He had about a year on patrol in Rotorua, having come via the Auckland nick where he had five years in the service. and he was singled out by the Big Boss for transfer over to us at the CIB. He would have to be careful as far as the senior lads in the office were concerned. He would have to prove he was no snitch for the Big Boss before he would be accepted as one on us.

When we arrived on the scene, a squad car was already there, and the Squaddie was busy putting up the SOC tape.

When we went inside the house the Victim was in a chair and her hands were tied with Duct tape. It may have been that she had tape over her mouth as I thought some of her makeup had been removed in a tell-tale fashion. It was nice and well-kept place. I have a theory that a tidy mind is like a tidy place so I can often tell as soon as I walk into a home what the rest of the house will look like. This was a well organised girl's place. I reckon she was one of those that was in charge of her life. You know the type. On a steady career path and the like.

I had a look and then let Mike have a look and see what he came up with. This was his first murder, but not his first dead body, so he handled it quite well.

At the door we conferred on what we had spotted. I started with "Mike, always look at the scene before you actually enter. It can tell you so much and that's before you start climbing all over the place with your size 10's and messing up the crime scene."

Mike was first. "No forced entry so she possibly knew him. Hands tied up with duct tape. Still dressed up so she must have recently got home. What have you got. Boss?"

I must admit that the idea of being called the Boss had some appeal, but I reckon my Boss would have knocked that on the head, so I compromised." First off, it's DS and not Boss. Second, you haven't mentioned anything about the cause of death. Understandable if she hasn't been shot but it's still something to think about. Thirdly, if you take a look at her mouth, I reckon she has had some makeup removed by force. Does that make you think she might have had tape on her mouth, and it was removed? There's other stuff that we could do. Estimate the time of death. Is there a strong smell of booze. Has she been drinking? If you think she has then often a push on the sternum will give you a whiff. No. it's not pervy when we do it as part of our investigation.

We agreed she had been drinking so then we queried where the nearest pub was to check if that's where she spent her last night. We'd drive by the Mitchell Downs pub on our way back. It was only up the road 100 meters.

The Ambulance lads were waiting to pick up the body, so we gave them permission. With a bit of luck Mike would have the Autopsy before the close of day.

We had the fingerprint lads in already and the photographer had already been and done his stuff so we had a look around the outside of the place. There was nothing to suggest the Victim had not been overpowered at her front door so that is what we went with. After that we knocked on the usual ten doors across the road and then five doors either side. Nobody seemed to know the Victim. She was one of those who kept to herself.

For whatever reason we decided that the Boss should also have a look at the scene so we left the Squaddie in charge and said we would be back later with the Boss for a second opinion.

Going up to the Mitchell Downs Pub it was confirmed that the Victim had indeed spent her last night at the Pub. The Barman, after asking around, reckoned she was a regular at the pub and 'probably lived around here somewhere'. When asked what time she had left the pub the Barman got onto the phone and spoke to the guy that covered last night's shift and confirmed she had left around 10.00pm. it might have been a little later but definitely well before chucking out time.

With that we went back to our new offices. The Sarge was busy trying to organise his cubicle with little success. He was trying to sort out ten years of paperwork into a space around twenty-foot square. If I do say so myself, the Sarge is something of a hoarder when it comes down to pieces of paper. Knowing the sarge he would probably take it home to annoy Huia but as always "you never know when I will need that piece of paper."

The Boss was trying to make head nor tail out of his space. Yes, he had an office, but it was only around twelve feet by sixteen feet. Maybe half the size of what he was used to. I knew that going in he would not be in a great mood, but I had to ask that he come in and have a look at the scene of our latest murder.

He was at that 'very frustrated stage' so when I went in, he immediately dropped everything and walked out to my car. He actually just walked right past me as he went towards my car. He was teed off with his new office and probably realised he would have to either dump some of his rubbish of he would end up taking it home and storing it there. He wasn't in a talking mood on the drive up and with Mike Jackson in the back seat he was definitely not going to say anything that would possibly reach the ears of the Big Boss.

Getting out at the crime scene the Boss stood at the gate. "You reckon an intruder might have got in. He probably surprised her when she opened the door. He stood over there, by the Hydrangea bush. She must have left the gate ajar for him to have easy access. Let's go inside."

I asked the Boss why he reckoned the intruder stood by the Bush. He whispered to me. "Disturbed crap from the bush. You can see the foot marks where he pushed himself into the bush. And obviously you spotted that one, right?"

"Obviously."

"Well done." Nodding to the Squaddie the Boss went inside the home. "Victim was found where, in the chair? Did you find out how long she had been at the pub last night?"

"Probably a couple of hours."

"Probably a bit the worse for wear, then. Victim was surprised by the assailant at the door. Note the angle of the door mat. There was something of a struggle out there and then she was brought in or forced in and shoved into the chair. Probably he then taped her mouth shut while she was still in a state of shock at being surprised by his entry. Do you have a time of death or a cause of death?"

"No. Hopefully we'll get a call from Mike this afternoon from the morgue. With both."

"Right. Everything happened within a few feet of this spot. Nothing missing from upstairs? Purse still around. That type of thing?"

I was surprised at how thorough the boss was being. Perhaps it was for Mike Jackson's sake. I continued. "No signs of a burglary that we can work out. Woman was a bit of a loner. We have not seen anyone who would claim to be a mate. Had a knock round the doors locally but no one seems to be a mate of hers."

The Boss was winding down now. "Well we do need someone who can tell if anything's gone. Looks like you and Mike will be putting in a bit of overtime tonight. We do need someone who can say if there's anything missing. Oh. While you're at it go up to the pub. See if she was with anyone last night. That place is full of locals so it shouldn't be too hard. You might buy Mike a beer. You can always put it on your expenses if you think you can get it past me."

With that the Boss walked back to the car and waited for me to unlock it. Mike got in the back seat, and we made our way back to the Station. Mike had been quiet the whole time we were with the Boss. Either he wanted to learn from the Boss or he was indeed a stooge for the Big Boss. I would later learn that Mike was eager to learn and he could not be called a stooge for the Big Boss.

The Sarge had given up on fitting everything into his space and was busy piling up boxes that I reckoned would find their way home.

The Sarge and the Boss and Mike Jackson and I sat and discussed the case. Going over the facts of the case we struggled to find any motive. Jealousy, perhaps. Burglary didn't seem to be a starter. We were going over the case when Mike from the Morgue rang. He had the prelim report for us although the Toxicity screen wouldn't be back until tomorrow. The three of us got into my car and we headed off to Mike's Morgue.

The Boss was already inside as I stood and locked the car doors. It's odd but when he is in this kind of mood, the Boss is usually set for his clearest thinking. He also does not tolerate idiots when he is in this mood.

I caught most of what Mike said. For the rest of it I would read Mike's report.

Mike Jackson looked visibly upset at the casual nature of the half-opened body on Mike's slab and went a little green at the gills. Mike Myles suggested he may like to leave and not puke on his clean floor. Mike Jackson left and stood by the car. The Boss did a little fist pump in the air. "Got him. Little sod was too good for his own boots. Sorry, Mike, you were saying?"

Mike grinned and continued. "Time of death between ten and midnight. Cause of death Strangulation would be my best guess. Hyoid is broken but I'll wait for the Tox screen to come back before I confirm that. Victim had a bit to drink prior to death. Other than that. A fit healthy young lady who I'd put down as perhaps late twenties to early thirties. I've seen her before, somewhere. Where did she work or live?"

I added my bit. "Lived in Goldie Street. No idea where she worked until we can find someone who recognizes her."

Mike reckoned he knew her from somewhere but couldn't quite place her yet.

We got back to the new office and the Boss, and I waited until it was after 5.00 to go home. We knew the Big Boss would be keeping an eye on us until he got bored so it was better to play it safe and leave after 5.00 O'clock.

I picked Mike Jackson up at his place at 6.30 and we hit the streets around Goldie Street. With in a few minutes we found someone that knew the Victim. Victims name was Eleanor. Didn't know the last name. Now we had to persuade her to come and identify the body tomorrow, and more importantly they had to come across to the Victims place and see if she noticed anything that was missing. The 'friend' had only been to the Victims place a couple of times, so she wasn't that much help. She didn't see anything that appeared to be missing so we left it at that and arranged a time for her to come in and identify the body at the morgue. Then we went to the Mitchell Downs Pub and asked a few questions. Yes, I bought Mike a beer and no I didn't try and get it past the boss as expenses. Getting back to the victim, she was a local at the Pub. Probably came in two or three times a week. Usually left with a bloke but on the night in question she was a little the worst for wear, so she walked home alone. She had been chatty with the locals but seemed to want to get drunk tonight, for whatever reason and had been a little the worse for wear when she left. She varied her nights in the pub depending on when she had a shift at the local Miter 10. With nothing much else to gather we left the pub, and I dropped Mike off and went home.

Wednesday

I was in at my usual time of around 7.40 and the Sarge was in just before 8.00. Even the Boss beat him in. The library café had closed down when the new Boss at the Library had brought in a cart for the patrons to order coffee from, inside the library. We had been lucky enough that that café had closed down just the week before we had moved. I don't know what it is about Winter, here. The days are much nicer than back in Manchester, but it still doesn't do me that much good when the clocks go back in April or whenever. Perhaps I prefer the lighter nights. Or it might be that I am just getting a bit older. I remember that I did try Skiing one year with a girl I was going out with. It wasn't for me, and I really can't see what all the fuss is about. Rotorua is not too bad when you get a sunny day. And today was fairly sunny.

The Boss was walking around and brandishing a newspaper and he was not happy. The newspaper had stretched the truth quite a bit and with supposition on their part had blamed the Cops for not having it solved already. We, that is the Sarge and I, knew not to react when the Boss was on a rant. The new lads were all ducking for cover and trying to look busy. I figure they will get used to the Boss's rants.

One thing we were missing was decent cup of coffee to start the day. The Coffee at the Café upstairs in the new Station was pretty poor and smelled of instant coffee. We left it to the Sarge to sort out a new coffee place as he did like a good coffee to start the day well. As for the sarge, he was walking round like a bear with a toothache. Like I said, he did miss his morning coffee!

There was still papers to be filed in every cubicle, but the Boss called a meeting and we all sat around, minus our cup of decent coffee, and discussed the events of the day.

The Boss took charge of the meeting. "Right, first things first, Sarge you have to do something about coffee for these lads. I really don't want to have to sit and see their miserable faces for the rest of time. Secondly, we have a murder case. Our first murder in the new offices so let's get it done right. Detective Sergeant. Did you get anything from last night's door knocking?"

I could happily reply with, "Yep, Mike and I got a neighbor who will be in in today to see Mike at the Morgue, and she should identify the body. Also we went to the Local pub. She is a regular there and she has been known to pick up a local to spend the night with. She works at Miter 10 so we will be in there to have a chat with them today."

The Boss seemed pleased we were making some progress. "Well done. Knocking on doors still pays off. Right now we have to sort out these damn night shifts. Before I start saying you and you are doing them, do we have any volunteers? Well, don't knock me over with your enthusiastic response."

No one made a motion to volunteer for the night shifts or the weekend shifts.

"Right, looks like we'll be doing it the old-fashioned way. It won't start until next Thursday night. So let me put Tim Cross on the 4 to 1.00 shift. Dave Powell will do the Midnight until 9.00am shift. It should be fairly quiet, and you can always ring me if you have anything difficult. I've been told I'm not to take part in the shifts but as a balance I have to be available as a backup. If you can't get me ring the DS, in fact you're better off ringing the DS if you have a problem. I'm told I can get a bit grumpy if I'm rung in the middle of the night. Yes, it's a complete mystery to me as well! I'm suggesting that we try this out for the next few weeks. The DS and I and Derek and Mike will be covering Monday to Friday inclusive. And Alan here, will cover the Wednesday to Sunday shift inclusive."

Everyone except Dave Powell thought it was an idea we could try for the next four weeks. Dave didn't want his Sundays off interrupted by having to work to cover the office. He agreed once it was agreed he would not be on permanent nights. He did have the experience that he could work on his own so that was plus for the Boss.

The Boss continued." Obviously, we will be trialing this set up. It may well prove to be a waste of time covering the midnight till 9.00 shift. If I don't hear anything from you lot that's what we will go with and try it for a month. Right, if nobody needs me, I'm in my office trying to fit twelve years of paperwork into five yards of space!"

The neighbor had already been into the morgue and identified the body as her occasional friend which left Mike and I to head up to the local Miter 10 and see the Boss.

The Boss's name was Phil, and we got a good reception with him. We asked a variety of questions, and he answered them frankly.

"Yes, she was a good worker. Usually helped out in the gardening section. She could lift a heavy bag, so she was well fitted for that job. Occasionally she helped out across the store as she was quite obliging. Full name was Eleanor Jane Mycroft. Born in 1995. No, she didn't have any great mates in the store, that I am aware of. Oh there was Jackie. She works in Gardening, but she didn't seem to mix that much with any of the store's people. No, she didn't go out with anyone from the Store. I tell a lie, she did go out a couple of times with the retail manager, John Bradbury but I was led to believe that fizzled out after a while. Been here for about six months though it might be longer. She had family in the North Shore as I recall."

We thanked him for his time and then went to see the Victims mate, Jackie, in the gardening store. Jackie was only young and got quite upset when we told her about Eleanor. I blame myself a little because Mike told her about her mate, and he just blurted it out. There are ways of telling bad news and Mike hadn't got that bit well covered. I'll put it down to the fact that he was fairly new at this type of thing. Once we sorted Jackie out, she was fairly informative about Eleanors private life. It seems that Eleanor liked to live on the edge and would often take blokes home that were a bit iffy. Jackie was a much quieter type of girl and I think she lived vicariously through Eleanors adventures. To myself I thought that would explain the place being so tidy and well organised. She would have to have it tidy if she was occasionally bringing a bloke into her bedroom for a one night stand.

Our next suspect was the Retail Manager, John Bradbury. I didn't really take to him, and I let Mike do most of the talking. John was something of a sleaze bag. They had gone out a few times, way more than the two times that Phil thought had happened. John was out purely and simply for the sex, and it seems that Eleanor did not mind that too much. They had had an argument a month or so back and split up. Despite John's best efforts to rekindle the relationship, Eleanor had been adamant. They had not really spoken for about two months other than work related stuff. I couldn't detect the hint of any residual anger in his voice so I couldn't count him as a possible suspect.

Going back to the office I wondered what my next job was. Obviously, I had to get the Local lads in the North Shore to go and tell the parents about Eleanor, which is what I did. My next job was to prepare a whiteboard with the details of the case. There was not a lot to prepare. Victim name, photo, address and after that I was struggling for details. She had only lived in her rental for about five months and had kept pretty much to herself. She went to the local two or three times a week. Occasionally, she picked up a bloke from the pub but there was no real consistency or habit patterns I could pick up on. All this was done under the watchful eye of Mike Jackson. He was keen to learn, and he let me do my thing with the whiteboard uninterrupted. After a while I found it unnerving, so I asked him to go and get the Tox screen from Mike at the Morgue.

It only took him perhaps twenty minutes and he was back watching me! I took a good look at the Tox screen. Signs of getting drunk last night. Not overly drunk but still a little under the weather. Other than that she was a healthy and quite fit young lady. The exercise she got working in the garden store would have helped her remain fairly fit.

I got a call from the grieving father at that point. I was tempted to let Mike handle it but I couldn't do it. It required tact and Mike had not developed those skills just yet. I spoke to the father, and I diverted his questions as best as I could. Firstly I had nothing to really say that we were on top of the case and secondly, I never gave too much away about the case. He had already been onto the Funeral director so left him with the planning of the funeral and I agreed to meet him when he got down to Rotorua.

I walked into the Boss's office, and he told me to sit down. Closing the door he returned to his chair and said, waving his arm at of the mess, "This is all because you pissed off the Boss."

We had had this discussion on several occasions, so I gave him my automatic reply, "And you didn't piss him off?"

The Boss replied, ironically "Let's say we both pissed him off. Any news on the murder?"

I filled him in on the lack of detail. "Victim was aged 28, worked at Miter 10, often went to the local pub and got a random bloke to take her home for sex. Father I've spoken to, and he is very upset. On his way down from Auckland. I think he's coming with the mother but he didn't mention her. Other than that I have nothing. She was a stranger to most of her neighbours so that's no help. She's only lived there for about six months and kept herself to herself. No motives to speak of and no enemies of note either. Not a lot to play with at this point."

"Someone will come out of the woodwork. They always do. Have you spoke to the Boss yet?"

"No. something tells me he is avoiding me. Maybe you will have some word when you have your weekly meeting?"

"Maybe. He's been nothing but business since we last had words and that was six weeks or so ago. Oh hell speak of the devil!"

I got up and left the Boss's office just as the CI swept into the room. With a hearty hi ho to everyone in the room he went into the Boss's Office and shut the door.

He was gone within five minutes and the Boss followed him out into the CIB room. The Boss announced that the CI was pleased that everyone was entering into the spirit of the move so enthusiastically and it was a temporary pain but well worth it in the long run. I have to say that the Boss delivered his speech in a monotone that reflected everyone's mood, so it got a laugh and then we all got down again to sorting out our cubicles.

Mike Jackson sidled up to me. "Er DS, what do we do now? About the murder case?"

I welcomed him to the realities of life in the CIB. "Well we have the Morgue report in place. Plus the Fingerprints and photos. We have been to see everyone that will have any input to the case. What do you suggest we do next?"

He was beginning to stutter. "Well we haven't done that much. Surely there is something we should be doing?"

"Like what! We can go out and stop everyone on the street and ask them if they did the murder or, alternatively we can sit on our arse and take care of general CIB business until something comes up with the murder case that we can act on. It's your call!"

It was then I realised I was being hard on the lad. He was used to seeing the shows on TV where everything happened inside an hour, less the commercials. I sat him down and had a word with him. "Welcome to the world of the CIB office. We can only act on crimes we get in. Trust me when I say half of the crimes never even reach our door. Then we can only go along and deal with the reports. After that we sit and wait for something else to happen. We are a reactive agency and occasionally a proactive agency. "Have you checked the fingerprints on the database yet?"

"No."

"Well do that. It will keep you busy for an hour and out of my hair. After that, go and have a wander around the secondhand shops. There are a number of them that are not above fencing a few stolen items. What you should do is go and introduce yourself to them. Tell them you are the new lad at CIB. Ask to see their recent buying records. Have a squint and say 'um Hmm' a few times. Then say you will take a look around if the boss doesn't mind. Half of this job is being seen around town. One day I'll take you to see Ronnie and Shi Low. Till then you have work to do."

Mike, I was warming to. Maybe he wasn't a spy for the boss. He certainly did have the right attitude. He was getting to the point where I was beginning to hope he was not a spy for the Big Boss. I was quite getting like him and his whole attitude.

By the time 5.00 rolled around I had my space pretty much in tidy order. I wasn't a hoarder like the Sarge or the Boss. I went home on the dot of five and had a lazy evening alone.

Thursday

The Sarge was still looking at coffee options for our lot and it might have been after 8.30 when the Boss appeared from his office with a piece of paper in his hand. It was hosing down outside, and it made me happy that I could do most of my work in the comfort of my cubicle.

"I reckon this might have something to do with your murder. It doesn't ring any bells with me."

It was a photocopied page with the word HARLOT written on it.

The sarge was walking past and commented it could be related to my case. Mike Jackson was now at my desk and made the comment that it might be a religious nutter.

The Sarge turned around and came back to my desk.

"Do you know anything about this lad?" He addressed his query to Mike.

"No."

"Left lots of clues, has he?"

"Er no. Sarge. Left us nothing to really work with."

"Do you have any idea what you are going to do? Today? to catch him?"

"No, sarge."

"So he hasn't left any clues, we have no motive to work with and we are basically waiting for him to do it again and hope he makes a mistake. That about sums it up, does it?"

Mike was looking a little sheepish. "Yeah, that about covers it."

"Then don't call him a bloody nutter. At the very worst we can imagine him as a religious fanatic but if he is smart enough to leave you lads guessing he's anything but a nutter. Think about it, lad!" With that the Sarge wandered off to whatever he was doing.

Mike was afraid he had pissed off the Sarge, but the Boss laid it out for him. "We meet with some of the finest criminal minds in our line of work. We also meet with crazies. I think the point the sarge is making is that you don't know whether this is a crazy or a brainy sod. So don't prejudge them until you are sure. You'll get used to it once you have been here for a while."

Turning to me, the Boss then asked. "So why did he call her a harlot? What does that even mean?"

The Sarge was returning from what he had been doing and leaned over the wall of my cubicle. "A harlot generally means a woman of easy virtue."

"A hooker, then." asked the Boss.

"No, a Hooker would be generally referred to as a whore in the bible. A harlot is usually a woman of easy virtue. There's quite a difference, biblically speaking."

At first the Boss was tempted to have a go at the Sarge for knowing these phrases, but he thought better of it. "So a harlot is a woman of easy virtue, is she?"

Mike spoke up. "That would explain her dress sense. She was pretty much showing what was on offer when we found her."

The Boss turned to me and said. "Who phoned it in about the murder if she had no friends around? Who phoned it in and when was it phoned in. Find that out DS? You might have a bit more of a clue."

I got on the phone to the switchboard and asked the question. Fortunately we were still having problems with the new switchboard, so the call had been logged and recorded as per the old system.

It was a bloke that had rung in. He only spoke for about ten or twelve seconds. He sounded like a Kiwi. There was no trace of a phone number that he rang from, which was unusual with the Switchboard we had operating. I asked the operator to forward the call to me and I would keep it on file. It was something out of the ordinary for the operator, but she said she would do what she could.

I reported it to the Boss and Derek Hildebrandt said he would go and see what could be done. Evidently Derek was a wizard on computers and phones. He had been well known for it at Hamilton, but we were only just discovering his talents. With in ten minutes the call was logged on my computer and also on my cell phone. Being something of a computer phobic I was very impressed with Dereks ability.

It might have been around 10.30 when the Big Boss rang. He had been contacted by the papers to see if the Police had any comment on the latest murder in Rotorua. I reckon the Big Boss wanted to say something of value to the papers but all he got from the Boss was 'No comment' to them. We are pursuing all of the leads and when we catch him is when we catch him. Oh and you might also think about not mentioning the note we got in the mail today. It won't help our case if the world knows about everything!'

The Big Boss wanted more than that but that was all he was getting out of the Boss!

Chapter 2

The Judge had already selected his next victim or person that needed guidance. It was a Chinese lady named Tiffany. Tiffany set off for work around 9.30 every day of the week. She had an establishment of some sort on Barnard Road. It may have been a nail salon or something of that nature. Usually the clients were there for a half hour to an hour. The Judges beef with Tiffany was that Tiffany had had her breasts improved. Normally Chinese ladies were more modestly equipped at the top of their chest. And they were usually subservient to their husbands. Not only was Tiffany immodestly dressed she was also independent. Surely any Chinese lady would bow to her husband and certainly not dress so immodestly. The Judge did consider that Tiffany may not even have had a husband. If so, she should definitely not go around dressed so provocatively. It was almost asking for trouble, on her part. He had discovered her salon, if that was what it was, on Barnard Road while he was doing his normal business. On following her to her home he discovered that she lived on Gordon Road in the Heights. She definitely wanted some guidance in her life and the Judge was the one to offer that guidance. He followed her home that evening and he was disappointed to note that Tiffany had three children of Asian parentage. There was no sign of a husband but seeing the three children greet her when she arrived home gave the Judge some pause for thought. Perhaps she would be spared, thought the judge. It would be terrible to wake the children up as he was chastising the mother. Even if she was dressed inappropriately perhaps the judge would leave her alone until the children grew up a little more. There were so many women dressing inappropriately it was almost too difficult to know where to start. But Tiffany would get her guidance from the Judge. Just not today.

You know how you get a good team all working together and then the team splits apart. That's what happened to us at the CIB. The First thing that happened was that Dave Powell decided it was time for him to get real and start his career path as it should be. He went to see the Boss and closed the door for a heart-to-heart chat with the Boss. The Boss eventually called me in and the three of us sat down to chat. It seems that Dave had decided to go for the next step and study to become a DS. The Boss called me in, and the three of us had a chat. Firstly Dave had to become a senior Constable which involved studying and an exam. He had decided that being on the night shift was a great time to do his studies. So far so good. The Boss told him that if he wanted to go for his DS exams he would be up for a transfer. Dave was accepting of the Boss's decision, but the Boss was happy to work with me as a DS so if Dave wanted to go the extra mile, he should be aware of the probable move. We discussed the move and decided that Dave would probably complete the exam within a month if he put his mind to it. Going onto the Night shift was perfect for Dave, so he left us and promised to send off for his papers for the Senior Constable step. That gave the Boss an excuse to remind me that I had said I would do the Senior Sergeants Exam and how was I doing with that?

Obviously, I had done nothing so the Boss told me I should be getting started on my papers if I ever wanted his job. That was probably the spur that I needed, and I came out of his office and set about signing myself up for my Senior Sarge exam.

It was the Sarge that mentioned we may have an issue. It seems the Hospital were getting a few cases where the injured person had broken a finger. It seemed to be happening with a little more frequency than usual. Obviously it was a coincidence but Mike, at the Morgue had been having a cuppa with some of the A&E lads and it had been something of a topic of conversation. The Sarge immediately thought of Shi Low. Were they getting a spate of shoplifters in their shops?

I said I would have a word with Shi Low the next time we had a cup of tea. I would mention it to him if I could find the appropriate words to use.

The next day I was asked to go into the Boss's office again. This time I had Tim Cross on my side of the desk with the Boss on his own side. The Boss started by nodding at Tim.

"Tim has been approached by a private security firm. If he is on permanent nights, they want to employ him on a casual basis as security for out-of-town VIP's. There are a couple of things I wanted, which is that he cannot work on a Thursday to Sunday, and they are happy with that. Secondly, I would want him to be available for any court appearances he may have coming up and they are happy with that. As I understand it, he would be licensed to carry a concealed firearm and it may only be one day a fortnight, but he assures me it will not interfere with his Police work. Do you have any further thoughts?"

I didn't have any more thoughts, but I did ask what he was likely to get for a day of Private security.

"I'd probably clear $500 a day if you don't object."

"So who would you be protecting?"

"VIP's mostly. Visiting heads of state. Politicians always get a local guy in to spot the local hot heads. Maybe a popstar or celebrity if they want to come down for a day or a concert."

I had no objections, so the Boss wished him well and reminded him that his first job was always with the local CIB. Nothing should ever interfere with that.

Once Tim had left, the Boss and I commiserated. "So it looks like our two boys have grown up and won't be available for the daytime."

In a way I was sad to see Dave and Tim leave the fold, but I did have the sense to realise that it gave us a chance to push the new DC's to see how far they would be advanced. He asked how the new lads were doing. I had to admit I liked Mike Jacksons attitude. He was keen to learn and kept his mouth shut when he was not being talked to. I reckon he was not a stooge of the Big Boss but that was only a hunch I had. Derek was already proving his worth as a whizz kid on computers. I thought that Hamilton would really miss him as he was also showing good promise. Alan Kirk we were both on the fence about him. He hadn't really showed an aptitude for the job. Some guys are meant to be on the beat for their lives and some are cut out for CIB work. With Alan I didn't hold out much hope for him ever doing CIB work but that was only my thoughts. The Boss was still on the fence with Alan. Only time will tell.

The Boss asked me how the murder case was developing. "It's something of a dead end. We have the Victim. But we have no motive unless you want to go with the 'Harlot' paper. No suspect and a lot of nothing in the way of leads. I don't go with the ex-Boyfriend at Miter 10 so after that, Zip!"

"Something will turn up. Even if it's just another body. They will make a mistake. They always do. Anything on the Arson lad?"

Nothing to speak of. Both of the schools are in the middle of getting the classrooms torn down and ready for the rebuild. Western heights should be done by Christmas. There are two at the other place. That may take a bit longer. Maybe March before they have the grand opening."

"What about the Arsonist. Any leads?"

"No, nothing yet. No prints to work with. He's getting better at lighting the fires so we don't stand a chance of him turning up as a corpse. He's probably due to have another go. It's usually a week or so between jobs. Maybe this week or next week before we hear from him."

With that I left the Boss's office. Mike was waiting for me as I emerged. He wanted to know if there was anything he should be doing. I told him that sitting and waiting was all part of the job of the CIB. I decided I would introduce him to Ronnie and Shi Low as people who could be useful. I had no intention of introducing him to my CI's. If you have read my previous stories, you will know why.

Just then the Father and Mother of the murder victim turned up. I was all set to sit them down with the Boss as he always deals well with that type of secondhand victim but as the Boss declared, I had the lead on this one so it should be myself and Mike! It would be good for Mike to learn that side of being empathetic with grieving parents.

They always want to know what we have achieved so far, and it was hard for me to spin that out into making it look like we were doing everything. Fortunately I remembered a trick the Boss uses. Get them talking about the victim or the funeral and they will want to speak about that. The Boss called it deflection. I called it a useful trick!

The Funeral was on Tuesday, and I said we would be there. The mother asked why, and I fudged my answer, but it was surprising how often the Murderer came to a victims funeral, Don't ask me why, but it does happen. We got down to talking about the relationship the victim had with her parents and it seems like they might have parted on a note of disagreement. Father had an argument with the victim about getting on with her life and not spending all her time at the pub. One thing led to another, and the girl headed south to Rotorua. I did say to Mike Jackson afterwards that the father could be a problem with his associated guilt trip that led to her death. I am beginning to sound like the Boss when he talks about his degree in criminology and criminal traits. We got rid of the parents around 10.00. That sounds a bit harsh, but it doesn't do for the police to get emotionally involved. It's a crime that wants to be solved and we needed a level head for that. Not to become emotional about the situation.

I rang Ronnie and Shi low and arranged a time to introduce my new colleague. Ronnie suggested we come round now and Shi Low we arranged to see at 3.00.

It was almost an anticlimax seeing Ronnie. When we got there I had to explain that if we turned up unannounced there would be a vehicle parked across the inside of the gate to stop us gaining access for a minute, which would give the Mob time to arm themselves. It somehow seemed tame to explain this to Mike. It almost sounded like I was trying to make it sound more dangerous than it was.

Going upstairs to see Ronnie I was greeted with my usual handshake and Mike also got a handshake.

I explained to Ronnie what the purpose of our visit was. I also explained that it was normally a fortress but because we had rung ahead, we were safe. Ronnie understood that I was trying to express a sense of fierceness about the gang. But Mike was chuckling a little. Until Ronnie pulled a Semi-automatic Glock 14 out of his belt and pointed it at Mike with his steady and unwavering pistol grip and the muzzle pointed at Mike's head.

"Me and the Sarge have a special relationship. He always rings first unless it's serious business. If he doesn't ring first, this is what they will meet! Don't you ever forget that. You are in the business of catching crims. I am in the business of being a crim. It won't always be this friendly."

Once Mike had clearly received the message, I asked Ronnie to holster his gun. Straightaway, Ronnie was back to his usual cheerful self. "So how you going, Sarge? I hear you got a murder up our end this week. I live one street over in Blomfield. Bad business when it gets that close to your house. Any leads?"

"Nothing yet. Seems the victim was a local who kept to herself. Went to the 'Downs' once or twice a week but other than that, nothing."

"Phah, I might have met her! I go in Mitchell Downs for a beer sometimes. Ah. You'll catch the feller, you always do!"

We chatted for a few minutes more. I was pleased to see that Mike now seemed to have a more perceptive grasp on the situation of meeting the Mongrel Mob. When we left Ronnie shook hands with Mike and said he was pleased to meet him. Always good when the Police brought their new lads around to meet the local crims. I couldn't help but notice that Mike's attention was well fixed on the gun that Ronnie wore on his waist. He'll get used to it!

Going back to the nick, Mike was quiet before he said "That was serious, about the gun and stuff. How can they be so casual about guns?"

"It's a part of their life, Mike get used to it. Oh and always ring before you go and see Ronnie. As you can see, it is appreciated."

We headed back to the Office. I have to stop saying that! We headed back to our new offices at the new nick on Fenton St. It was time for lunch, so I had a subway and sat with the Sarge. He was busy telling me about a new coffee machine he had spotted in Noel Leeming's. If we all chipped in a couple of hundred, we would have enough for the machine and also a variety of these new coffee pods he had heard about. Made it easy to sort yourself out with a decent coffee. If we all chipped in, we could get one of these machines. I had other things on my mind so I might have said that I would be a starter for the machine but it was just one of those throwaway remarks you make to end a conversation.

That afternoon we went to see Shi Low. I again gave him a walk past and asked him to say what he saw. He was a little more on to it in that he said it would be easy to defend and the stairs were not wide enough for two people to go up at a time. He said he assumed that the door could only be opened from the inside. I have to say I was warming to Mike Jackson. I hoped he would not be the Big Boss's spy in our office as I quite liked him and his potential.

We went up to see Shi Low. At first Shi Low wanted to speak with me alone but when I mentioned the reason for my visit Shi Low formally welcomed Mike into his office as well. As always it was a formal meeting, and we were offered a cup of tea which was poured for us by Shi Low. It may have only been for ten or fifteen minutes, but I did feel that we were honoring Shi Low by introducing Mike to him and that Shi Low also appreciated our gesture. I broached the subject of a rash of finger injuries and I was impressed at how Shi Low maneuvered Mike out of the office, leaving him and I to talk amongst ourselves.

Shi Low asked me to explain what I meant by a rash of finger injuries at the hospital.

"There have been at least five instances of someone breaking their finger accidentally. That is something of an unlikely coincidence in the space of a month or so."

Shi Low fixed me with a stare. "We are alone Detective Sergeant. If you prefer we can speak a little more directly."

"Thank you, Shi Low. Is it possible we may be experiencing a possible spate of shoplifters in the businesses owned by your people? You have a modest reputation for not bothering my colleagues when you get bothered by these trivialities."

"As you say, Detective sergeant, we do not wish to bother your colleagues with every small piece of shoplifting we come across. My people have many businesses in town and it would surely be an inconvenience if you were called to every offense of this nature."

"Shi Low. If I may speak so bluntly. All of the injuries at the Hospital have been concerned with the breaking of the last finger of the hand. That is what I mean by it being too much of a coincidence. I would be disappointed if that was due to the Influence of you and your people. My colleagues would esteem it an honour if your people and my people could work together to remedy this small occurrence."

"Detective Sergeant, I will bring any such matter to your attention should this ever happen again. However I do not foresee such an event. Now, if there is nothing else to discuss, I should get back to my business."

I had been dismissed with just sufficient rudeness to know I had been chastised but also to know I was a welcome visitor, if I behaved myself as civilised people could expect to happen. Well, whatever happened I had made my point to Shi Low himself. I suppose I could count that as a win.

On our way back to the Office I told Mike that only other people he would need to meet were the Elders at the Ohinemutu Marae. I explained that I wasn't the best person to make the introductions and the Big Boss would probably do that at the appropriate time. I had had a bit of run in with some of the elders on the marae and I wasn't sure whether they had forgiven me, yet.

Mike asked me to look at one of the secondhand shops he had visited on the way back. He had a concern about some item on sale, so we popped in and checked the registry of sellers. It seemed above board but full marks to Mike for thinking it may be dodgy.

Friday

The Boss called us all in on the Friday to advise that from the start of next week we would be starting the new Shift roster. "Right, so Tim and Dave Powell will cover the two nightshifts. They won't be in until Thursday night. Alan will cover the weekend shift, so he won't be in until Wednesday morning. The DS and the Sarge and I will cover the Weekday shifts along with Mike and Derek. Any questions?"

Alan was a little nervous about covering the weekend shift since he was such a Newby. The Boss had an answer for that. "Don't worry, Alan. The DS will cover the Saturday with you, and you won't be on your own until the Sunday. Right, any other questions? No? Right then. Get busy and enjoy your last weekend off. From Monday we're all on to it."

With that the Boss disappeared into his office The Sarge decided he would bring up the topic of the new coffee machine on Monday and he went off to his Cubicle. As for me it was just 9.00 and I found myself with nothing to do! That also meant Mike and Derek had nothing to do and probably also Alan Kirk.

I told Mike and Derek and Alan to start reading old case files. If there was anything with fingerprints available, they could run them down on the database. For me I caught up with the papers. Both local and national. I hadn't had a good look at them for the best part of a week and it filled in my day to the point where I didn't notice it had turned 5.00 until the sarge nudged me that it was time to go.

I thought I had a game of golf booked in on the Saturday with the Boss and the sarge, so I confirmed the time as 11.00 and I went home.

Monday

It was odd coming in to start a new day at the new office. For a start I only saw the Boss and the sarge and Derek and Mike. Everyone else was having their time off due to the shift roster.

I'd get used to it!

The Boss called a meeting. Other than the Sarge having a dig about the coffee machine we actually had virtually nothing to talk about. My murder case was going nowhere. We really were waiting for this bloke to commit another crime and hope we got some clues to work on. Mike and Derek had nothing to do, and the Boss was one of those lads that gets peevish when he has nothing to occupy his mind. Over the weekend we had an armed robbery for smokes at a dairy. I hate when they start a trend like that. Call me a pacifist or whatever, I hated it when an armed robbery happened for something as stupid as a packet of fags. Or in this case a whole swag of fags and vapes and lighters etc. Due to the Boss's inactivity it was decided we would all go and have a look at this armed robbery. Within a few minutes we were all into the Boss's car and heading to Springfield Corner where the robbery occurred.

The Boss and Derek interviewed the victim while Mike and I went to the neighboring shops and asked the owners if they had noticed anything dodgy. One of the shops was a pet parlor and they were bleating on about the state of crime in Rotorua. As they were not exactly in a high crime area and definitely not in a high crime type of business, I left Mike to deal with them while I went next door. There was a Dairy and a pet parlor, two food shops which wouldn't be open until 5.00 and a cabinet maker who had a factory in Riri St.

Mike and I went to see the Cabinet maker and I quite enjoyed driving the Boss's car. Very flash, these BMW motors. With all of the bells and whistles you would expect. I wondered if I might consider one of these BMW jobs until the Boss told me the price later on. I would stick with my Mitsubishi, thanks!

The Cabinet maker had nothing to add to our report. The Incident had happened at 3.30 on the Sunday afternoon so everyone around had been closed. We drove back to the Victims place and were surprised with Derek. He had been allowed to take over the security camera of the dairy and he got a heck of a lot more than I had seen from a security camera before. By cross analyzing something with something else we actually had a fairly clear view of the number plate of the offenders. By analyzing this and cross-checking with the Station we were able to say that the car had been stolen.

It seems that the offenders had parked outside the front door of the shop with their engine running. Driver in the driver seat and two passengers had got out wearing masks or scarfs. They had rushed into the shop brandishing what looked like a sawn-off shotgun and demanded the attendant fill a couple of bag, or backpacks, with fags and vapes. There had been a second attendant, so the second robber had demanded the second attendant empty the till. There would not have been more than three hundred in the till, and it did seem like a second thought to those of us who watched the tape back at the office. Within perhaps three minutes they were out of the shop and into their getaway car and zooming off into the distance. The first attendant had been a little slow in filling the backpack and the robber had pushed him aside, violently, and taken over the job of filling the backpack as quickly as he could.

When we got back to the Shop, the Boss was asking how much had been taken and the owner was estimating around twelve grands worth in total. When the Boss looked at him with that disbelieving face of his, the owner amended the total to perhaps nine thousand dollars' worth. The Boss still did not believe him but said he would be crosschecking the shops purchases with the sales. It was something they had to do with every burglary, the Boss said, which was news to me. At which point the owner reckoned it was at least five grands worth. The Boss wrote five thousand dollars in his notebook and snapped it shut. "Thank you for your help, Arthur. I will file the report and give you an incident number for the Insurance. Let me know if there is anything else to mention and I will let you know if we find anything."

Getting back into the Boss's car, he groaned and said. "You must be a right shorty, Detective Sergeant." Pressing a button on his centre console the seat smoothly went back to its original position. When I didn't bat an eye, the Boss said simply "It's something you get in a Beamer. It comes as standard, I think. Does your motor not have that?"

I didn't dignify his comment with an answer.

On going back to our new office we set up the video feedback and watched the whole robbery occur. In and out in under three minutes. Derek reckoned the thieves might be amateurs as the second robber had not asked the attendant to empty the Lotto Drawer. There would probably be a grand in there by midafternoon on a Sunday. There were three people in the shop when the robbers entered, and one had quickly got out of the door and the other two were hiding beyond a shelf end. Could they give us a description or be of more help to us? The Boss reckoned It was something that Derek and Mike could pursue so he sent them back to the shop again. I have to say that the new office had all of the bells and whistles we had struggled for at the temporary offices. Video phone, okay, that didn't work that reliably. Top of the line computers and instant access to our database of crims. And we had fiber connections which were ten times faster than what we had put up with. We felt like we had been given a whole new set of tools to play with. That is to help us catch more crims, obviously.

Derek and Mike got back to the office with a couple of leads to chase up. No one had thought of grabbing the witnesses to the robbery and they had fled the scene. But we knew what they looked like so we should be able to get them to come in.

After that the day drifted on until 5.00 and I went home. My study papers had arrived, or the first set, and I determined to read them that night. I got sidetracked by something and forgot about the papers, so I ended up watching something and nothing on the Telly.

Tuesday

In at my usual time, the sarge had splurged on a coffee set which was to be only for himself or anyone else that fancied dipping into their hard earned notes and chipping into the purchase. Somewhere along the line I had agreed to chip in, evidently, so the coffee was also for me once I chipped in my two hundred. The Sarge is a mate, so I did chip in, and I have to say the Coffee was very smooth. At less than a dollar for a cup I was quite happy. Having the new machine installed the rest of the gang also chipped in their two hundred so the Sarge was not out of pocket. Come to think of it, he might have made a few dollars on the deal!

At 9.00 the Big Boss rang. The papers wanted a comment on the string of armed robberies happening in Town. I am afraid the Boss was not overly polite to the Big Boss. As in "what are they talking about! It's just the one armed robbery only, and then the Owner is trying to do a dodgy with the insurance. Tell them to sod off until we do have a crimewave happening."

With that he hung up. I'd have said that the Boss was in a grumpy mood, but then he picked the phone and dialed the Big Boss. "I have a story you can do in the local rag, and it makes me, and you look good. Are you interested?"

I assume the Big Boss replied in the affirmative and the Boss said he would be right over and fill the Big Boss in.

And that is how the Boss and the Big Boss featured in a story about Rotorua getting tough on crime.

It stemmed from the Big Boss's demand that the CIB were now to cover pretty much all our busy days and nights. The fact we didn't cover all of the nights was glossed over, but you get the picture. With the help of the Boss it turned into a story about Rotorua Police getting tough on crime. The Boss was interviewed, and the Big Boss was also assisted by the Boss in setting up the story. Needless to say it became about the Big Boss deciding enough was enough and 'didn't the citizens of Rotorua deserve a top class police force' etc etc.

Somehow the Big Boss was coerced into saying that anyone wanting answers to any Rotorua crime should ring him first. I think he may have got a little enthusiastic or that was what my Boss egged him on to say. Nonetheless it was out there in print!

At 11.00 Mike and I went to the funeral for the murder victim. There were a few from Miter 10 and couple of the local neighbours but it was a quiet funeral overall. There was nobody at the Funeral that had me interested so I put this down as a nonevent. When we got back to the station it was lunchtime, so we had our lunch and Mike and Derek were off in one corner trying to do something with the computers. I filled in time until it was near enough to five and I went home.

Chapter 3

The Judge was Impressed. They had a new minister at his church. This guy was not a minister, He was a preacher! He really knew his stuff. On Sunday the sermon had centered around the 'mark of the Beast'. The minister had talked about how the mark of the beast was everywhere. The mark of the beast was of course a euphemism for the mark of the devil and it was everywhere! The minister had spoken about how they were using the mark of the beast in their everyday signage, but it was so subtle you had to know where to look for it. In every barcode there was a 6 at the beginning and a six in the middle and a six at the end. And of course the mark of 666 was the sign of the beast or the devil. The minister had asked every member of those present to get out their wallet or purse and take a look for themselves. He was so right. There was a mark of six at the beginning and a six in the middle and a six at the end. The minister was so right. When he next went to the dairy he checked and the 666 was on all of the barcodes on every product. Yes, this was a sign of the end times when the mark of the beast was everywhere. He vowed there and then to only use his card when he could not make it to the bank to withdraw money from his account. He had to go to the bank today and when he got to the head of the line, he was amazed at how the teller was dressed and flaunting herself so provocatively. Yes, she was generously endowed but the brazen manner in which he was served was outrageous. She was very familiar with him and even called him by his first name. There was not a doubt that the end times were coming if this was the loose standard in which even the bank tellers displayed themselves so brazenly. He wondered if this was another sign to him that this girl needed a lesson from him, but he was so shocked he just conducted his business and left the bank.

<u>**Wednesday**</u>

It made the news the next day and even the Herald had a brief mention of it on the following day. Today the headline read "Police Chief gets tough on Crime." There was a brief story on the front page and there was a full page story on page 6. Nearly a whole page and the Boss got a mention as well. According to the papers the Boss was the right hand man waging a war on the evils of crime in Rotorua and the Big Boss was mainly concerned with crimes against the citizens of Rotorua. The sarge had purchased a copy of the local paper as he liked to keep a scrapbook of anything concerning his area. When the Boss walked in, we were all reading it over the Sarge's shoulder and despite our raucous cries, the Boss described it as 'A load of Bollocks'. "It's what the papers wanted and it's a slow news day and it will be fish and chip paper tomorrow."

He did come over to get a closer look and we all agreed that it was a great photo of him in the rag until he realised the Sarge and I were winding him up. Mike and Derek kept quiet as they didn't know how far they could push it with the Boss.

One thing I was noticing was that the usual Monday/Tuesday and Wednesday crims were staying at their usual pace. I was looking forward to seeing how things would eventuate on the Thursday/ Friday/Saturday and Sunday shifts. The new DCs were working out fine. Although Alan Kirk was a bit slow on the uptake on his first week as part of the new squad, Derek and Mike were keen to do and learn what they could from us. Alan had started the first day of his new shift that day as he was working over the weekend. I rather thought he should be paying a bit more attention but that was only my initial thoughts. It seems the Boss was also having second thoughts about Alan Kirk.

"He's very good at surfing the web. I'll also give him full marks for reading the papers when he is at work." was the Boss's only comment as we got to lunchtime on Alans first day of his new shift. "Let me know how you find him on Saturday. It's never too late to get rid of deadwood in this job."

That was the Boss's comment, and I knew Alan was now on borrowed time to impress the Boss.

It was just after 2.00 when we got the call about another armed Robbery at a dairy in Hamurana. The Squad car or I should say cars, was already on its way when the Boss and Derek and Alan and I piled into the Boss's car and headed out to the scene.

And they didn't have cameras for us to see so we had to rely on witness statements. Fortunately they had managed to hang on to two witnesses. We went through our routine of interrogating the witnesses and the shop owner. Again the target was smokes and vapes. Again we had a number plate to report on and again the vehicle was stolen and had been for a couple of days.

The Boss was peevish that again the robbers had pretty much used the same MO as the previous robbery of a dairy. Sawn off Shotgun, two robbers got out while the driver stayed with the vehicle. There was only one attendant at this place, so the Robbers got in behind the counter and helped themselves while the second robber shoved the attendant to the back of the shop and forced him to show where the Cigs were hidden in the back room of the dairy. And he filled up another backpack with cartons etc. All done and dusted within three minutes and the Vehicle had shot off heading towards Ngongotaha. Within twenty minutes the squad car had found the abandoned stolen vehicle in a back road. Working things out afterwards, we decided that the Robbers had another accomplice driving another vehicle that was legitimate and they had made the swap over of vehicles in a backroad and then driven legally on the road while Cop cars were zooming all over the place trying to catch the robbers. It seemed like a smooth operation. We did have the fingerprint lads out dusting for prints at the scene of the crime and also at the stolen vehicle but if they were that smart, they were unlikely to leave prints anywhere.

When we got back to the office, we filled the sarge in on what had happened. Oddly enough the Sarge was a sounding board for us when a crime had been committed. He often had ideas about a fence or about a possible suggestion as to our first line of enquiry.

This time he had nothing to help us, so we sat around and discussed the case. Alan, Derek and Mike sat in the Boss's office along with Myself and the Boss and the sarge. It was too crowded so we all grabbed our chairs and moved to the middle of the office where we did manage to discuss the case. With me on the whiteboard, I wrote up the suggestions.

Organised. Someone said Well organised and that should be emphasised. The fact that they were nicking a motor a couple of days before showed they were well organised.

Stealing vehicles as a getaway vehicle.

Possibly a great market for cheap fags or baccy. Was that market in Auckland or here in town?

Also a good market for vape materials. Becoming very trendy with the youngsters.

Targeting Dairies was an easy mark. No big security issues and most dairies were owned by the guy that stood behind the counter for 12 hours!

Working in town and also outlying districts.

One target on Sunday and one on Wednesday. Did that tell us anything?

Is this an alternative to the ramraids we recently spoiled.

Is there a crime ring operating again. Maybe selling fags in Auckland?

These were the main topics which we then discussed. Without that much success I should add. It was new crime for Rotorua and, as much as we would prefer not to say it, we almost needed a few more cases to get a trend for what was happening. We brought up 5.00 and we were still discussing the case but eventually we all went home with our thoughts.

Thursday

Today was the first day of the new shift rotation at the new office. I suppose we were all keen to see what effect we would have on Rotorua Crime stats, and we were all waiting to see what would happen that night with Tim and then Dave Powell on duty.

For the lads on the day shift, the Boss and I went out to visit the crime scene again at Hamurana while the three DCs were told to act busy and eventually go out to the Pubs and clubs and see if there were any cheap fags on offer. When we got back to the office Mike and Derek had gone out to the pubs and Alan was manning the office. The Boss was not thrilled with Alan's work ethic, but he kept his mouth shut. The sarge offered to have a word with Alan but the Boss reckoned we should leave him alone and see how he coped at the weekend.

We had nothing to develop any leads on either the Hamurana case or the one at Springfield Road, so we were at a loss for anything to do. Derek and Mike came back and reported that there were no cheap fags or vapes on offer at the pubs. For the murder case we also had no leads to work with. Mike had run the prints through our database and come up with nothing. Derek and Mike picked up a GBH at the Mitchell downs that needed our attention. They came back with the suspect handcuffed and led him to the cells. Then they sat down to deal with the paperwork. The Boss and I made it through to 5.00 and went home. All in all a boring day at the office!

That night I got a call from Tim Cross. It was just after 11.00 pm and he had received a call out to View Road. When he arrived there he got on the phone to me as he reckoned I would be interested in the callout.

It seems that there had been a break in at the picture framers place on View Road. By sheer coincidence the business next door was an auto spares place and they had been getting their random nightly visit from the security guys when he noticed the back door of the picture framers was open. When he went to investigate the guy who had broken into the framers place was leaving after setting fire to the place. The Security guy had the element of surprise on him and had him down on his chest when he smelled something on fire. He got hold of the fire brigade and they put him through to the local copshop which is how Tim Cross had arrived and, within a few minutes, I was also on site. The Fire brigade were already there and had minimized the damage from the fire to the workshop only and were already rolling up their hoses when I got there.

The security guy had the offender in those plastic wrist bands and Tim had made the thing more certain with his handcuffs. He was locked in the back of Tim's vehicle and when I arrived he had the suspect in handcuffs, the Fire Service were rolling up their hoses. The owner of the Business was there and immediately recognised the accused as someone who had a complaint against the business that had not been satisfied.

I had a word with the Fire Service boss and he agreed to get his report to me by midday. Tim was called away to a case of GBH so I said I would take the arson guy back to the station and start the paperwork. I was already up and what did it matter if I wasn't back in bed for another hour or so? I could always have a lie in and come in late for the day shift.

I got the guy back to the station and charged him with the Picture framers fire. A part of me wanted him to confess to the other fires as well but he wasn't going down that road. I formally charged him with the arson on View Road and then went home. I also had the picture framer boss in and he told me he had a dispute with the offender a couple of days prior. Something about a frame being damaged and the glass broken and you could clearly see where the frame had been banged on the wall. The Framer had said it was not covered and the offender had gone away saying the framer had not heard the last of this.

I charged the offender and went home to bed leaving the offender to spend the night in the cells

Friday

Thursday night had been busy for Tim Cross. The arson case and a GBH for Tim to deal with and a domestic assault for Dave to tidy up in the early hours of Friday morning.

Having a couple of lads on duty who were familiar with the routine made it a lot easier for us and there wasn't a great deal to carry on with when I arrived in at 8.30am. I busied myself with the arson guy and Mike joined me for something to do. I had the guy for the picture framers place as he had been caught out leaving the place. Now I had to try and pin the other arsons on him. Mike walked off to his own cubicle before returning to mine. "On the day after the first arson our friend downstairs went up to the hospital on a completely unrelated matter. He reckoned he got burned when something at work exploded. He says he lost his moustache and eyebrows when it went up. The A&E reckon he also lost his hair on his arms and hands. Do we want to buy into that or does it want a bit more explaining?"

I had to say well done to Mike. He had done just a bit of digging at the hospital and came up with the info. It didn't necessarily place him at the scene of the fire but it certainly gave us reason to doubt him. I suggested Mike take a copy of his credit card and go to Mitre 10 and Bunnings. We knew the original petrol can had been destroyed at the first fire. Maybe the guy had been forced to buy another petrol can?

Mike was back with in a half hour. Our arson friend had needed to buy another petrol can at Mitre 10. We could now place him loosely at the scene of the second blaze. Yes, it may be circumstantial, but all we needed was to raise a doubt in the minds of the jury. And we had traced him because he was stupid enough to use his credit card. I was thinking about this and I reckoned I would make a great criminal as I wouldn't be making all of the stupid mistakes the average Crim makes.

I had a hunch and I went with Mike to Bunnings and Miter 10. I asked the guys there if you needed to sign anything like a poisons register when buying Weed killer. Unfortunately, the answer I got from the guy from Bunnings was a no. The guy said he would check if the guy had an account or a power pass card. Now we were in luck. The guy had indeed purchased a better quality weed killer and the dates were before the later of the two weed spray events. We went back to the station and I let Mike take the lead when we re-interviewed the guy. Mike was quite good in an amateur sort of way. He did get an admission the guy had possibly brought a gallon of the better quality weed killer for his gardening job. We left him thinking about that while we went for lunch. When we returned we laid out everything we had discovered about the weedkiller and then the petrol can and then buying a new petrol can because the first was now melted into a wedge of plastic goo in the first fire.

While the guy was watching us we discussed whether we had enough to charge him with all of the six crimes. It must be a little unnerving when the boys in blue start adding up how may crimes they will do you for. As far as Mike and I were concerned we were not bothered that the guy was keeping quiet as we added the charges together. We decided we had enough evidence to charge him with all six crimes, so I charged him with all six crimes and then left it to the CP to make the charges stick. My next job was to assemble all of the evidence we had on the offender. He did ask how he could make it all go away. Mike and I laughed at him. If he was done for all six cases, including the weed spray cases, the only way he could make it go away was by serving jail time. I told him they were being quite hard on arson cases at the moment, but if he wanted to confess to everything we would be sure and tell the CP. When I reckoned he would be looking at probably six to eight years for the lot he declined and said he would take his chances with the jury.

It sounds odd but sometimes it takes all of your mental acuity to solve a case. At other times you fall over a suspect. With this one we had rather fallen over the suspect but we never complained. As far as we were concerned it was another six crimes we had a suspect for and that is always a good day in our office.

The Boss called me into his office for a sit down talk and we both reckoned we were suffering from overkill as far as our manning levels were concerned. He congratulated me on the arrest of the Arson guy. I had to admit I had been lucky but the Boss was unperturbed. He reckoned we need the odd bit of luck now and then. Then we got to talking about our Golf game on Sunday, we were that bored and with nothing to do.

Saturday

I was in on Saturday along with Alan Kirk. Alan didn't seem to be that proactive, so I sat on the computer while Alan was sitting on his computer. At 11.00 we had a domestic incident to attend to. Alan stood around and watched me do my thing. It was the usual thing. She had been assaulted and he was being very penitent once the Cops were called. I knew we were not going to get a complaint from the wife so we urged her to go to the hospital for a checkup, which we knew she would not bother doing. We left the crime and went back to the office. At just after 2.00 we got another complaint at the same address, so we went in with a more determined attitude. I let Alan take the lead at this point. He arrested the guy and then went into the wife to get her to lay a complaint against the Hubby. He coped OK, but I knew it was a waste of time.

Once back to the station Alan went through all of the charge sheet without my assistance. I'd have to say he did ok but it was the minimum amount of effort that he put in. Just the bare facts without any embellishment that the CP could work with. On a scale of 1-10 I'd only give him a six for his effort and I reckon we needed a bit more than that.

Sunday

It's my day off and I have a golf game with the Sarge and the Boss lined up at 11.00. I didn't get a phone call from Alan, so I assumed he was having a quiet day at the office. I actually won the day with the Sarge coming second by two shots and Boss coming a distant third by another four shots. I enjoyed my beer at the Boss's expense and then I went home to mow the lawns. Surprisingly it was four or five days since I had received the Senior Sarge exams and I had done nothing with them. I sat down over my late lunch and gave them a look through. Surprisingly I was fascinated by the study set up. It was one of those exams where you read the papers thorough and then you get asked questions which account for half of your total. I knew I would have to read it a few times, but this type of study usually suited my style. The lawns did not get done!

Monday

The Judge was both pleased and a little perturbed. The Ministers sermon the previous day had been on the topic of 'Onanism'. At first the Judge had wondered what he was talking about, then it became clear. 'Onanism' is the practice of pleasuring yourself. The Minister had gone to some lengths to say that it was better to spill your seed on the belly of a whore than to commit the sin of Onanism. On a personal level the Judge knew he may have been guilty of this sin of onanism on more than a few occasions. Yet the Minister was saying it was Ok to spill your seed on the belly of a whore. It was not something he had ever done before but if the good book said it was ok, who was he to argue?

Later that week he did try the Ministers suggestion and it certainly felt very good and without the seeds of guilt he always felt when committed onanism.

Afterwards he did wonder about how the women who were religious handled the sin of onanism. Perhaps it was not something the woman should be ashamed of. The Minister certainly laid emphasis on the Males not committing Onanism. Perhaps it was ok for the woman? If he ever got that close to a person in his church, he would ask her delicately for anything in a *relationship with a woman should be discreet.*

In at my usual time and the sarge was busy making my cup of coffee. He quite liked the idea of being a part time Barista and I reckon he was getting quite good at it.

Dave Powell was still in the office as his shift did not finish until 9.00. He had a quiet night and he had been able to get in a good study session. We sat down with Dave and the Boss, and the Sarge and Dave reckoned it was something of a nonevent having to cover midnight until 9.00 from Thursday until Monday morning. There was nothing to do! At the very least, he was being paid to do his studying for the Senior Constable exam.

The Boss reckoned we would trial it for a month and then see what we wanted to do with it. While he was talking, he asked Dave how his study was going. Dave reckoned he would be ready for the Senior Constables exam within a couple of weeks if the Office for his night shift was as quiet as it had been.

I knew the Boss had a reason for asking but I didn't know what it was. Perhaps the Boss was looking out for the furtherance of his squad. Dave left to get a sleep. The Boss kept himself busy with paperwork and I had nothing to do for the day. Perhaps I should go and see one of my confidential informers? You know what I am on about, so don't be coy about it.

My Boss got a call from the big Boss. It seems that the application for a permit to carry a concealed weapon had just come across his desk. Was Tim cross leaving and why was he leaving? When the Boss said he was not leaving but was only looking for a part time job as he was committed to working the night shift as per the Big Boss's orders. Then the Big Boss started grilling my Boss about Tim being tired when he did eventually turn up for work. My Boss answered his questions, but it was a few more minutes out of his day. I believe the Big Boss did sign the permit for Tim to carry a concealed weapon eventually but his enquiries with my Boss had been so negative. I wondered if his whole attitude was based on that same sort of negativity. Then I realised that all of his interactions with me had been fairly negative so that maybe was how he handles all of his junior staff.

I decided to give myself a small treat so I rang my CI's to see if any one was available later in the day. I made the calls and Tiff was free that afternoon. I loosely arranged a time and then looked for work that would keep me busy until that time.

I was reading reports of trending crime patterns which was interesting if a little boring. Armed robberies of dairies was up by 32% and I was pleased to see that Rotorua was mentioned. There were no significant increase of these crimes being solved. It seemed that it was a case of wait and see if a trend develops. That wasn't much help, but it did somehow justify my own inactivity.

Sarge and I had lunch together. He was trying to tell me I should keep my left shoulder a little looser on my backswing until I reminded him that I had actually won yesterday's game. Maybe he was winding me up?

I had nothing to do until later that afternoon, so I struggled to keep myself occupied. The Boss was also struggling to keep busy. I rather hoped he wouldn't ask me to do anything later that day as I had other plans. He didn't. He kept himself in the office until four and then he disappeared. I left shortly after and went to consult with Tiff. She had nothing new to report but we had a pleasant chat for over an hour, well we managed to pass the time, and I went home.

Tuesday & Wednesday

It was another glorious late summer day and It was hard for me to look busy. I had nothing to really do. The CIB cases we had were going nowhere. Anything that happened at night Tim and Dave were handling quite efficiently. Alan came in for his shift on Wednesday, but he was happy surfing the web. According to him he was doing research, but the Boss and I were already thinking he was not cut out for CIB work. On Wednesday the Boss and the sarge and I sat down for a brew, and we all reckoned we needed a good crimewave to keep us busy or were we a couple of lads too many in the office.

Wednesday afternoon we had another call at 1.00 telling us there had been another armed robbery at a dairy in the Ford Block. Four of us went out to see the scene leaving Alan in charge of the office. It was the usual scenario. Three lads in a stolen vehicle. This time they were brandishing a revolver rather than a Sawn off shotgun. But it was a similar MO. In and out in under three minutes. I drove round the area and found the stolen vehicle in Hathor Street. The Fingerprint lads were busy at the dairy, and I sent them off to the stolen vehicle when they were done at the dairy. There were no witnesses other than the attendant and they had shoved him out of the way as they rifled the cigs and vapes and the till which would not have had any more than $300 in it. It was an interesting place the dairy at Ford Block. Most of their clientele were beneficiaries so a lot was put on the slate until benefit day. I think the Owner was most concerned that his book of 'on the slate' clients was kept by him and not taken by the robbers. The insurance would cover the Fags and vapes as far as the owner was concerned.

Leaving the Dairy we reconvened back in our office and discussed the case. We had learned nothing new and we were still back at square one. Did the fact that this gang used a revolver, rather than a shotgun, mean we were onto a new gang? I left the Boss with that thought and I went home at five o'clock.

Thursday

It was just after midnight that I got a call from the Boss. It seems there had been a sexual assault in Otonga Road with similar overtones to my murder case. Did I want to take it? I took it and got out of my warm bed decrying my decision to be in the CIB. When I got there to Otonga Road the Squad car and an ambulance were already there.

I walked in the front door and the Ambulance guy was just finishing off with the victim and she was saying she didn't need to go to

Hospital. Reluctantly he finished off while I was outside talking to the squaddie.

"She reckons she was letting herself into the front door when the assailant rushed up to her and forced his way in. He grabbed her and shut her mouth with Duct tape and then he tied her down to the chair. Again with duct tape. Then she reckons he must have just looked at her for a minute before he said to her that he was going to remove the tape from her mouth. She said nothing so he did that and then he lectured her for a quarter hour about the way she dressed and going out to a pub and listening to heathen music. When he asked her for her input, she reckoned she was going to reconsider her ways. He was saying she should go to church and stuff, and she said she agreed, and it was time to get her life back in order. Hang on, here comes the Ambo."

I asked the Ambulance bloke how she was, and he reckons she got off easy. She could have been raped or worse. She's fine and she doesn't want to go to Hospital so she's all yours. If I knew your rank, I'd use it. He said.

"Apologies. I'm DS Mark Hammell from the Rotorua CIB."

"Leading Ambulance man, Tommy Farlow. Like I said she's all yours. Mark. Good luck and I reckon she got off lucky."

With that he was off to his next job. I asked the Squaddie if he had called the fingerprint lads in, and he said that was for me to make that call. I left him putting up the scene of crime tape and I went into see the victim.

She was unfazed by the happenings or so it seemed. She offered me a cuppa, so I accepted, and we sat down at her table.

"I was coming home from the Belgian bar. They have a country music night on a Wednesday, and I usually go down. I opened my front door and then the sod was on to me. He bundled me inside and then I was tied up or taped up or whatever. He had a go at me about how I was dressed so provocatively."

"What did you say?"

"I agreed. If that was going to keep me alive, I was ready to agree with the bastard. He seemed to have a freak on about how I should be dressed, and I was asking for trouble dressing the way I was dressed. I agreed with him. In fact, everything he said I agreed with. After a while he seemed to have come to a decision that he was struggling with. He started talking to me like an uncle or a father. Said I was mad for dressing that way and all it did was drive men to a state of lust. I should be going to church and listening to the way of the Lord. I agreed with him, and he said he could see there was no need for further punishment if I kept to my word."

"Can you describe him?"

"Close to 1.80 tall. Medium build although he might be stronger than he looks because I was no match for him."

"Describe his face. Beard or moustache?"

"No, he wore like a balaclava even in this weather. Covered everything. I can't even tell what colour his hair was. He did have eyes that looked right through you. Like he reckoned he could see into your soul and that was where he was looking at."

" Okay, what about his accent or his voice. Pakeha or Māori or, I dunno Indian maybe?"

"No he spoke like he was reasonably well educated. If I had to guess his voice, I'd say Pakeha."

"No limp or anything else that might give him away. Left handed or right handed?"

"He tied the tape with his left hand and held the tape roll with his right if that's any use."

"Not really. Did he touch anything in the room?"

"No. he had gloves on. He had those; would you call them cyclist gloves but with the fingers still on them?"

"Okay, so it's no use getting the fingerprint lads in?"

"No, he was very careful about not touching anything. Always had the gloves on."

"No sexual assault? No peering down your dress or anything like that."

"No, like I said, I'd pick him as a guy that got God. You know one of those converted ones that take everything literally."

"Lastly, have you noticed anyone following you home recently. Maybe you saw him when he wasn't wearing his balaclava."

"I dunno. I never take that much notice of things around me. Usually I am in a hurry to get where I want to go."

"One last thing. How often do you go out of the evening. Once or twice a week?"

"Usually a couple of times. I work in a bank, and it can be pretty stressful with all of these Mortgagee sales going on. so I limit myself to a couple of times a week."

"Thank you. Nicola. Now is there anything I can do for you. you sure you don't need the Hospital?"

"No thanks, Mark. It's off to church this week for me!"

"Really?"

"Yep, until you tell me you have this prick locked up in a secure facility! He knows where I live, and he knows where I work! I live on my own and that makes me happy. You just tell me when he is locked up. Until then I might just change my lifestyle for a week or two."

With that I left Nicola's place and went home. I told the Squaddie to forget the tape. We had all we could get from this young lady.

I got in just after 9.00 and the sarge said he knew about my early morning call. The Boss was upstairs with the Big Boss, so I thought I'd wait until he got back to report on the assault or something like that. Yes, it had actually been an assault. He had manhandled her into the lounge. Whether it was a sexual assault was something of a call on my part. I went with the sexual assault because I already had a dislike of the guy, and it made it easier for me to be against this guy if he was also doing sexual assaults.

I had to work on the assumption that the two victims, last night and the murder victim, could be related. I worked on that angle for a while, but all I could come up with was they were both very attractive looking ladies and tidily dressed, if just a little provocatively. Other than that I couldn't get any connection between the two victims. I had to think. Were they dressed provocatively or was it just what they would call fashionable these days. With the benefit of hindsight I reckon they were being a bit more fashionable rather than being dressed provocatively.

That was my take on the situation. Maybe our religious fanatic held girls to a higher standard? That's another thing. He seemed to be only targeting the Females. Why is that. Someone had called him religious. Yes, that was Mike Jackson. Was that why he was going on about the way the girls dressed?

I was sitting at my desk when the Sarge bought me a great cup of coffee. I discussed the case with the sarge. As I looked around, I wondered where the other DC's were. In the Big Boss's office discussing the cases on our books, said the Sarge. The Big Boss had his phone ringing nonstop since the article in last week's paper had appeared. He wanted to get some of the pressure off him, so everyone had gone upstairs this morning at 8.30. It seems I had just missed the meeting. How sad!

At 9.30 the whole squad returned to street level and the hot topic was my sexual assault case or was it just an assault case? Whatever!

I explained about the case and the similarities to the murder case. The Boss asked me to continue looking at the murder case as a part of this case somehow made some sense. For a moment the Boss asked me to focus on just the Sexual assault case from this morning. I explained that the assailant seemed to have a fixation with the Bible and had urged the Victim to change her ways. Although he had not threatened her as such, I still felt the threat was implied. You know if she did not change her ways there would be consequences etc. The group seemed to agree with me. I then opened it up for questions. And there were several comments.

How did this lad know she lived alone. Had he followed her home more than once?

How did he know she lived alone?

How did he know there was not a bloke also living there. Maybe he had followed her on a few occasions.

How did he know where she worked unless he was a customer at their bank?

Why did the victim think he knew where she worked. Had he seen her as a customer? Or was he a customer of her bank?

Had the assailant actually gone to the Belgian bar and attended the evening as a fellow paying guest? Did the Belgian Bar have inside security cameras. Maybe the guy had been spotted by the cameras?

By opening up to the group I had a fair few new questions to ask of the victim and of the Bar. I decided I would start with the Bar. It was only a few minutes' walk away, so I strolled up and asked if they had cameras on the inside. Yes, they did! It was handy when they wanted to screen unwelcome guests.

I looked at the footage for the best part of two hours while the Barman/owner identified those he could. I asked the Barman if I could take the footage back to the office for them lads to see, no problems and he downloaded the footage onto a USB and sent me away with it.

Running the footage for the rest of the group was not that profitable. The Sarge was the biggest identifier of known crims, but he wasn't a country music fan. He did recognize a few faces and I feel we had identified over half of the patrons that night. Maybe I'd show it to the Victim and see if she could recognize anyone.

I rang the victim and told her I would be around this evening. She had taken the day off, so I was able to go up there and then.

We looked through the footage and I was more intent on watching her to see if the Assailant could be recognised. She identified a few faces as regulars but of the rest she was not that helpful. She did think that one or two could be a possible suspect but there was nothing definite. Well I had the footage so that was probably a plus. Returning to the office I went to the Boss's office and reported my findings. We had given it a go, but we weren't going to get any further with the footage.

The Boss suggested I stop thinking about the case for a while and asked me to check up on a few details of the Robbery at Hamurana. If nothing else, it brought up five o'clock, so I went home. I did study that evening for a couple of hours and felt just a little virtuous.

Friday

Was an odd day. It was one of those days where the world wants to catch up with you.

I had a call from the parents of the murder victim. They were leaving today for their place on the North Shore and rang into me in the vain hope that we had solved the case or got any new leads. I was about to tell them of the new case when the Boss told me not to. He probably had his own reasons for that, and I did forget to ask him.

I told the parents that we had no new leads, but we were pursuing the case with some urgency. They were happy with that reply and left their Motel and went home.

Then I had a call from Mike at the Morgue. He'd heard on the grapevine that we had another sex assault case. Would we be bringing a body in for him to work his miracles on? I told him no and that it was a sex assault case, but the victim had agreed with the assailants suggestions, and he had said she was a good girl if she did as he asked her. Mike seemed disappointed but he knew he would get any case we had. He was the official Morgue in Town!

Then I had a call from Dave Powell. It seems he wanted to query a question in his studies, and he reckoned I was the best guy to ask. It was something about the Crimes Act. As luck would have it I had studied the nearly identical question last night, so I could answer with some confidence. While we were chatting, he told me that the late shift at nights was really boring with no calls to speak of. He reckoned he wouldn't mind trying the South Island as a transfer if he passed his exam.

I reckoned the South Island was too cold for a lad from Auckland, as he was, and I told him I had a great time in Napier as a senior Detective Constable. He said he would think about it, and we left it at that.

Then I got a call from the Big Boss asking me how I had got on with last night's Sexual assault. I assumed it was because he's had a call from the local paper. I filled him in on all of the details that I could, and he said he hoped I would make it up to his office the next time he called for a CIB meeting. Maybe he called for the sex assault or maybe he called to give me a rollicking for missing his meeting. Either way I didn't really care. I answered to my immediate Boss, as far as I was concerned.

I didn't see anything in the following days paper about the Assault case. Perhaps they had other stuff to fill up their pages.

The last person to ring me was Janet. I hadn't been to see her for a week or so. I actually reckon she was being friendly and not pushing for business. Plus she and I got on quite well. Maybe she just wanted some sex!

I arranged a time with Janet for later that afternoon and I was surprised to realise it was just after midday.

I had my lunch with Mike and filled him in on all of the details of the sexual assault case. If two of us knew the details, it would be two brains working on solving it. Derek was working on the Boss's computer and trying to make it go a bit faster. He reckoned if the Boss would spend about forty dollars his machine would go about ten times faster. The Boss agreed and the next time I saw the Boss at his computer he was grinning from ear to ear!

Mike Jackson had followed up a case of GBH for Tim Cross earlier that morning. Tim had dealt with what had happened at midnight and

Mike dealt with the paperwork and a follow up enquiry. Between them they would make a good team.

I had a word with the Boss after lunch. He reckons he would give it a month's trial for the early morning shift. First off it would give Dave Powell a chance to finish off his Senior constable papers and set him up for the exam. And secondly the Boss had decided that Alan Kirk was deadwood that needed to be set free from the CIB office. Overall, I reckon the Boss did not want to rock the boat until Dave was ready for his exams. He was good like that.

It was a quiet afternoon and I really struggled to fill in my time until I went to see my CI Janet. Yes, the whole concept of having the office attended was a great idea in theory but in practice we were well overmanned and with having the cases dealt with as it happened, we were actually struggling to fill in our days. Even the Sarge looked a little bored. He was close to asking the Beat lads if they wanted any assistance.

I hadn't been told I was up for a Saturday shift, so I left to see Janet after checking with the Sarge we were still on for a game at our usual time on Sunday.

I had a conference with Janet which lasted a little over an hour. Nothing much to report and nothing to really make a note to the Boss about.

Chapter 4

The Judge thought that the Minister had been in particularly great form on Sunday. His sermon had centered on the story of Jezebel. Jezebel had married Ahab who was an ancient King She had forced Ahab to bring in a rival god called Talbert. Talbert was a nature god worshipped by her father who was a priest. When it came down to a face off whether Yahweh or Talbert was the better god obviously Yahweh had won but Jezebel had shown all of her feminine wiles to influence the decision which displeased Ahab. Jezebel was forever etched into the Judge's mind as a woman who would steer a lover into the worship of a false god. Indeed she was one of the first feminists as she was defiant about the worship of Talbart who was actually a woman. It was the first time the judge had really thought about the story of Jezebel. He now had a new category for females. They were either a Harlot or a whore or a Jezebel. If they were pious, he would call them an obedient servant but in today's society there were so few, sadly, who made it into that category.

Monday

A miserable winter's day. On the upside I had won the game on Sunday, again. The Sarge and the Boss had tied for their spot, they called it equal second, but I kept referring to it as being equal third. It kept the Sarge on his toes. I was having a good run, having finished with a 101 which was three shots ahead of the others. Going into the office I was keen to hear how Tim and Dave had got on with their weekend shift. I suppose I was also keen to hear how Alan had fared but to be honest I didn't hold out much hope for him as a future CIB lad.

The Sarge made me a coffee and we had a meeting with the Boss and the Sarge and I and Dave, Derek and Mike.

Alan had pushed a couple of assault cases over to the day shift for us to handle. He had been busy with an armed robbery of a tourist place out at Waikite. It didn't seem like it was another case for the lads who were doing the Armed Robberies at the Dairies. The Boss was not thrilled but it was for him to sort out Alan. I am beginning to agree with the Boss that Alan may not be cut out for CIB work. But it is up to him to make that call.

Dave had had a quiet session on his shifts. On the upside he had made great strides into his studies so the Boss was keeping quiet on that front. Tim had been fairly busy, and he had a couple of things for Mike and Derek to follow up. Mainly witness statements for his GBH case and a few follow ups for assaults at various pubs. It's odd how you seem to have a spate of one type of crime then you won't get any for a month or more.

The Boss also handed me a letter from the guy with the murder and the sexual assault case. It was the usual single page letter with the word 'SAVED!' on it. It sort of confirmed that the guy with the murder and the Sexual assault were the same bloke. Again it was photocopied so there was not a lot we could do with it. The Boss said it if had been posted to us was there a chance we could go back through video footage and see who had posted it. He handed that off to Derek and Mike to follow up. We didn't realise how much of a haystack we were looking into. Derek and Mike were very good at following up the leads and within a day we had a couple of dozen security tapes to go through. Here's the rub. Most shop owners are more concerned with their own security and that is where the cameras were aimed. There was only one camera out of the whole bunch that had a glimpse of the postbox outside the shop. It was not one of the Boss's best ideas, but it did keep Derek and Mike busy for a couple of days. The Big Boss put in a call to the Boss asking how we were doing with the murder case. We assumed it was because the papers were asking but the Boss was being positive in that we were following up every lead we could.

It was not until Thursday that we had another case to work with. Two cases actually.

Thursday

Again it was just after midnight when I got the call from the Boss. "There's been another murder. Looks like your bloke again. I'll see you up there!"

This murder had been committed in Sunset Road. I got dressed and made my way up there. The Boss was already there along with the squad cars and an ambulance. He met me on the roadside. "Same as the others but this time the bird is dead. She's young. Probably been to the pub or somewhere. Dressed up nicely but still dead. Come on. Let's do it."

I followed the Boss in. I noticed that the gate was ajar. The Boss was ahead of me. "Same MO. Looks like he rushed the bird when she was fumbling with her keys. I dunno. Maybe he was standing there by the magnolia bush while he was waiting." There was a large magnolia bush in the middle of the lawn which was why the boss had surmised that and there were trampled fallen flowers on the ground. It's a thing you notice when you have been doing this job for over ten years.

By now we were inside the lounge.

"I'd guess he rushed her in, she's a bit drunk so her reflexes are not sharp. Before she could react, she was all tied up with the Duct tape again. Let's have a guess that she gave him a bit of lip when he started having a go at her and he decided to top her. Killed by choking her, I'd say. Any thoughts?"

"Sounds about right. I can smell the booze on her, so she has had a drink. Nice and neat. No other damage or sign of a big struggle. She is dressed for a nice night out so is she dressed provocatively? I wouldn't have thought so, but I am not the one to judge. Okay. Let's get the print lads in and then we'll have a look and see where she worked. There doesn't appear to be any robbery motive, so it does look like our lad has struck again."

With the two of us being there we were a lot more thorough. There was no robbery that we could see. The fingerprint lads were thorough and once they had finished, we went through the property with a fine toothcomb. That's just a saying, by the way. It means we were as thorough as we could be. An hour later the Ambo arrived and took her away.

I asked, "Who phoned it in?"

"One of the neighbours was walking their dog and noticed the lights were on and the curtains were open. When he looked in, he could see she didn't look right so he called it in. He lives up the road. Do we want to go and get him up again?"

"We should do. It is a murder scene!" If I am up, I don't really care about others getting their forty winks. It's a part of getting old and cranky I have been told!

We walked up to the neighbor who had reported it in, and we had to knock him up. He wasn't thrilled but he did at least offer to make us a cuppa while we chatted. His Missus was all up in our face and asking her questions. Maybe she was the town gossip and wanted to get it all firsthand?

The Boss quietened her down and we set about talking to the bloke who was walking his dog.

Nothing unusual to report. He was taking his dog for a walk, and it was unusual to see a light on and a curtain open at that time of night. He estimated he had walked the dog about midnight give or take a few minutes. He said the girl looked a bit odd. The position she was in seemed a bit odd. So he ventured to walk on her lawn and saw that she looked like she was dead because she had her eyes open. That's when he called it in to the 911 service. It was now a quarter to three in the morning, so we thanked him for his answers, and we closed the door with the Squaddie on guard at the scene and went home.

I got in at 10.00 and the Boss got in just after. The Sarge had heard from downstairs what had happened so we were not expected to be in at our normal time.

I was just sitting down for a coffee when the phone went. There was an armed robbery in progress out past the Airport. We knew they would be gone before we got there so the Boss sent Derek and Mike and Alan out there while we finished our paperwork. We'd be out there within a half hour.

When the Boss and I arrived at the armed robbery we were greeted by the three DC's who had the Scene of crime tape up. The witnesses were lined up. The owner was lined up and a list of stolen items was already available. Stepping back I motioned to the Boss that this is how all crimes should be. Let the lower minions go out and do the hard yards and let the Boss's come out later when everyone is lined up and ready to speak to you. The Boss agreed that if it was a perfect world, all crimes would be this way but it's not perfect so enjoy it while you can!

We went through the witnesses and the owner. In and out within a few minutes. I went and drove round the area. I found a stolen car within a couple of miles parked by the river rafting place by the café there. We had the Fingerprint lads out, but it was a waste of time there were no prints! I went back to the scene and the Boss reported that it was the usual MO. Stolen vehicle. With a backup motor stowed away somewhere. They had got in and got out within a few minutes. The Owner said they had a sawn off shotgun they were waving about. We had a couple of witnesses, from the local resort, said they had not really seen anything as they had got their heads down behind a shelf. We did have a video of the crime which we would look at when we got back to the office. Other than that it was another armed robbery with nothing to go on. Cigs and vapes had been the target as usual and they had opened the cash drawer but only got away with a few hundred dollars. Oh, and one of the robbers had grabbed a stack of chocolate bars as they went out.

That's probably what I would have grabbed if I was in their place.

We had a situation where we had two crime scenes to examine. We let Mike and Derek and Alan sort out the armed Robbery while the Boss and I went back to the murder on Sunset Road.

It looked quite different in the light of day. We gathered that the girl worked in a local Post office. There were no indications why she would have been selected. We canvassed the neighbours who were all up with the state of play. Perhaps our witnesses' wife had been the bearer of all of the bad news. The victim kept herself mostly to herself. She went out occasionally to the Pub. She used to frequent the Citizens club in town. Once we got someone to put themselves forward to identify the Body, we could then get official confirmation of who she was. We had one neighbor who reluctantly came forward to ID the Body. Victim was one Angela Sorstedt. Lived alone. Aged 26 Ish. Worked in a local Post office on Pandora Ave. we did ask if she had parents or anyone who would be bothered about her demise. It seems she was alone as both parents had died. Didn't have a boyfriend but she was quite popular at the Citizen club as a friendly girl. There was no connotation attached to her being friendly. She was just that type of girl.

The Boss and I went back to the office and put our thinking caps on. This was the third murder in about as many weeks. All we had to do now was wait for a letter to arrive in the post and we knew it would probably be the same villain.

We were no more well advised as we had been with the first victim. We had him as a religious fanatic who saw it as his personal mission in life to teach youngish girls the error of their ways. I still had the ideas from the meeting up on the whiteboard so the Boss and I and the Sarge looked over them. We still had nothing to go on and this lad wasn't leaving any clues for us to pick up on. Maybe we should go and see Nicola again and see if she had remembered anything we could use.

The Boss teed us up to visit Nicola again on the Thursday evening. He picked me up at 7.00 and we went to see her. She was pleased she had not made the papers. We told her that it was probably because they had other stuff to print that was more newsworthy. She thought that molesting her was pretty damn newsworthy, but the Boss managed to persuade her that the forthcoming byelection in Auckland had probably kept her off the front page and isn't that what she wanted?

We got very little out of Nicola, until we told her about this morning's murder which we hoped would be the same guy. After that Nicola started to cry when she realised how close she had come to being topped. The Boss motioned me to go and comfort her Which was not my cup of tea. She calmed down eventually, and we let her alone. The Boss and I went for a beer to Mitchell Downs pub, and we discussed the case.

"It should be in all of the papers tomorrow. Rotorua has its own serial killer. Can you see the Daily Post letting that one slide?"

One of the locals walked up and asked if we had any success with the murder. We said not yet but we are working on it.

Then the local guy suggested we broaden our search. What about someone who meets a lot of people. A courier driver? Bank worker? Postie? What about a dairy owner? They know everything that goes on in an area. What about a chippie owner? They know everything going on as well. It certainly sounds like someone that knows the area if the girl in Goldie Street is anything to go by.

The Boss thanked the guy for his input, but he would have preferred not to be reminded of our failure while we were having a beer. The Boss said "And that's why we have a bar at the Police Station. So we can enjoy a quiet beer without other idiots bending your ear. Come on Mark, Lets go home. We had an early start this morning. Shall we say 9.00 in the morning?"

Friday

I took advantage of the Boss's offer and got in just before 9.00. Again, it was hosing down, and I was looking forward to a quiet day in the office. Maybe a meet with the Boss and see if he had come up with anything on our murder case. Come to think of it I was fairly well involved with the Armed robbery mob as well. That's the perks of being a DS. When the lads can't think of what to do they start hanging around and asking if you have suggestions.

The local newspaper had come out full bore with the suggestion that Rotorua had it's very own serial killer. Yes, there was coverage of the new murder, but we really had copped it as a Police force by having a serial killer that was eluding the police at his whim. It might sound crazy, but these killers do not outwit the cops. They are fortunate if they don't leave a clue lying around. This guy was smart and wearing gloves, so we had no prints to work with. All we ever wanted was a clue and that would give us something to work on. The Big Boss had been contacted, after his article the previous week. He had got on to the Boss who had nothing to say. The Boss got on to me to come up with something we could use as a quote. I could only say that all avenues of enquiry were being pursued. The Boss inserted the word 'Actively' into my quote and between us we managed to get something together that the Big Boss could say. It helped in some ways that we could say we were not giving too much away as we were actively pursuing our enquiries. Then the Paper asked for comments on our other enquiry, the armed robberies. The Big Boss was pleased that he could sound just a little pious and rebuke the reporter for being so unfeeling at the time of a murder in our city.

It was around 10.00 when we got the call. A dairy in Ngongotaha was being held up but by now they had well gone. Our role was to interview the witnesses and file the prints for the database. We took Mike and Derek and went out there to have a look. Usual MO. In and out inside of three minutes. They did have a go at the till and got away with best part of a grand. It seems that a lot of the locals used their tick allowance and quite a few had been in on the Friday morning to settle their accounts. Smokes and vapes had been the target and the owner had been out to AWL the previous day and stocked up with Smokes. The Boss reckoned there would have been the best part of fourteen grand gone plus the cash. The Owner of the dairy was livid. It was always a good day for him on Friday and he had been hammered when he was most vulnerable. For the Boss and I, it was simply an insurance claim for the owner to tidy up and we were more concentrating on catching the crims. We interviewed witnesses and the owner and then we caught up with Mike and Derek. They had found a stolen car on Parawai Drive so everything looked like it was the usual gang we were no closer to catching.

When we got back to the office, we were all soaked and just a bit smelly, so the Boss suggested we all go home and change our gear. It was appreciated.

While I was home, I got a call from Janet. She had rung the office and told I was at home, so she rang me at home. I had spoken to Janet the previous week and during our talk I had mentioned we were looking for a religious fanatic that was doing murders and yet one girl he had let off when she said she was going to change her ways. She said she had a one off customer that fitted our bill. She said he had been in and done his thing but all the while he was saying how this was under the Ministers express orders. She told me how he had said it was better to spread your seed on the belly of a whore than the other option. Janet had never been called a whore before and part of her was pleased at how sexy it sounded and part of her was teed off at being called a whore. She was doing it because she loved the idea of sex with random strangers. Yes, I know it might sound odd to you, but she was happy, and they could afford it and the extra money she could spend on herself. Janet also explained to me that she had not thought it could be a minister of the crown as this guy sounded like a religious person and they did not go usually into politics.

I said I'd call round later to see her, and she immediately put the other connotation on my meaning. So why not?

At 11.00 I had got a call from Mike at the Morgue. It seems he had a full report on the last murder victim and If we would wait for another couple of hours he would have the Tox screen back. This was unusual for Mike. Usually we would have a preliminary report the same day. But I did agree that we could wait for another hour or so and then we would come and get it. He seemed assured that we would come and get it rather than wait for the Courier to do his thing and we would not get it until the next day. The Boss and I went to the morgue, and it was close to midday before we got there. Mike was acting all official and making us sign for receiving his report. The Boss asked him what was going on. It seems that my Big Boss had spoken to Mike's Big Boss and complained about the delay in getting a tox screen back. Mike's Boss had said words to the effect of 'Stuff them. They can wait until we have everything for the report' and only then could Mike release his report. The Boss went to see Mike's Boss and somehow everything was sorted out and we would be expected to have Mike's report as per usual. While the Boss was away, Mike gave me the gist of the report. "Female aged 28. Death by strangulation, you can see the marks on her neck. Probably used just his bare hands. She'd had a few drinks, but she wasn't boozed up. Time of death somewhere between 11.00 and 1.00 in the morning. He went into other details but that was what I needed to hear. It sounded very much like the previous Murder. Same MO, so we were probably looking for the same guy.

We drove back to the office, and I went in to see the Boss. I remembered that I had a call from Janet and he said it was fine for me to go and see her. He did ask if I would be taking Mike Jackson with me. I looked him straight in the eye and said probably not. I'd prefer to let the new DCs contact their own Criminal informants. He kept a straight face. His reply was to the effect that I might as well leave Janet until after four O'clock and then I could go straight home. I don't know who won that one, but it might have been a draw!

The sarge teed us up for a game of golf on the Sunday at our usual time so I went over paperwork for a few hours and then went to see Janet and we had a great talk. She wasn't a whole lot of use with the religious fanatic. She had been keen to get it over with once she pegged him as a fanatic. It was only later that she thought of our recent conversation and gave me a ring.

I asked to see her cell phone as I was keen to see if she may have got the phone number of this guy. Unfortunately it came up as a private number so that was a nonstarter. For me it gave me something to think about. How many local vicars had recently given a talk on casting your seed into the belly of a whore? It was something for me to think about on Monday. I settled in for a quiet weekend, not forgetting our game of golf on Sunday, and I again did some studying for my senior Sarge exam. I have to admit I was enjoying the study. It gave me something to think about other than the murder case.

It's an odd thing that happens with your brain. You try and keep everything in it's own compartment to keep them separated but you might be thinking of the ram-raiders when you have a random thought about the murders. You almost have to make a conscious decision to switch your brain over to the murders for five minutes as your last thought could be important. Unfortunately for me I had one of those brains where if I let it, my mind would keep swapping over to the problems in my head and trying to connect them all together as one big problem. A girl I went out with once said I had a girly brain as that is how women think. I called it multitasking which is when this girl said exactly! I don't really know but it can be a help, sometimes.

Sunday

It was generally heavy showers on Sunday. We went out and played our game. I lost big time as I was struggling to get a good grip on the club with all of the rain. The Boss and the Sarge both got 102 each and I was somewhere north of 110 shots. I paid for the beers with good grace. It would be hopefully someone else's turn next week. The Boss asked me how I got on with my CI which was quite tactful for him. The Sarge immediately said. "What, has Janet had a session with our murderer?"

I didn't quite know how to respond to Sarge's comment, but I did say that Janet had been as helpful as she could. The Boss and the Sarge exchanged a knowing glance. I finished my beer and went home to dry out.

Chapter 5

M**onday**

The judge was well impressed with the new minister. This week's sermon had been on the topic of swearing. He actually used some swear words as a part of his sermon. The older members had been a little upset but when he revealed why he was using these words, they understood completely. He used several examples to explain his topic. It's a common expression 'Gor blimey' until you realise what it stood for. "May God blind me for I have seen a beautiful woman and I have had sinful thoughts." The Judge could imagine people having sinful thoughts when they saw a beautiful woman. He himself had been tempted on rare occasions. The 'F' word was filled with obscene connotations and the phrase 'Bugger me' was an open invitation to participate in homosexual activity.

The Judge thought he knew most things, but this was astounding to him. He was convinced they had used the last phrase in a well seen TV commercial. It might have been said by a dog but was that an invitation to Bestiality. He was amazed at how these phrases seemed to have just slipped into general usage. Last week the sermon had centered around the end times. Was this just one more example of how depraved the world was becoming?

How come on your weekend off its pouring down and when you have to go back to work, the day is gloriously Sunny?

I was reflecting on that, when the Boss collared me on the way in. "Hey. I've been thinking about what you said yesterday. Is it worth having a ring round all the local vicars and see if they have given a talk on casting your seed to the belly of a hooker. There can't be that many would pick that as a topic for a sermon. It might pay to try some of the staucher churches. It's the type of thing they would go on about."

Once I got inside, I set Mike and Derek to have a ring round the churches. I set them off and quickly realised that in most Churches the Monday is a day off for the vicars or whatever they are called. I told them to flag it away until Tuesday. The Sarge came and had a word with me. He had heard the DC's having a ring round and he was suggesting that we might consider expanding the terms of search. It seems that in the Bible the act of pleasuring yourself is also called 'onanism' we should try tomorrow and use the word Onanism. Best not to tell Mike and Derek what they were talking about. It could be embarrassing for them. I could see the exact moment when they realised what Onanism really meant. It gave a bit of cause for mirth in the between calls.

It would have been around 11.00 that we got a call from a dairy in Sunset Road. They had been robbed and it sounded like our gang of lads. The four of us went to the scene of the crime and quickly got into our usual roles. I followed the Boss around while Dave and Mike took Mike's motor on a search for the stolen car. They found it on Blomfield St which was handy to Ronnie's Home address. I might go and have a word with him later on. The usual MO. In and out in three minutes. Smokes and vapes being the target. They had also had a go at the till but there was less than a couple of hundred dollars in at the time. We did get some grief about this being a regular occurrence in Rotorua and what were we going to do about it. The Boss fobbed them off by replying 'we are asking these questions. What are you lot doing about it?'

Then the reporter arrived from the local paper. He got into it with the Boss and came off second best. Yes, she would have her story, but I couldn't see the local Police being painted in a good light.

We went back to the office after leaving the Fingerprint lads to do their magic. When you do something like a dairy with a hundred or maybe even a thousand customers a day it's not only boring as you have to do the prints, but there are also so many prints to deal with you tend to only go where the robbers touched or you would be there all day.

We looked at the video of the crime and then we looked back at the previous video from out in Ngongotaha. On first they had used a sawn off shotgun. On the second they had used a revolver. The more we looked at the robbery scenes the more we came to the conclusion we were possibly dealing with two gangs! Somehow the villains looked different when we compared the two videos. The Boss was not thrilled with this discovery. The sarge looked at the tapes and he also came up with the same conclusion.

That night we got our first breakthrough on the case of the Armed robberies. A Mufty squad car was heading up Otonga road and he phoned in a suspicious vehicle. For those of you that don't know a Mufty squad car is when you have a car without all of the Police writing on the side. It's the vehicle they use when they are out chasing speeders on the highway that suddenly flashed blue and red lights at you when you have been caught. Usually it's painted a medium blue or red and designed to blend into traffic.

The suspicious vehicle was parked in the dip just beyond the first rise in Otonga Road with three occupants and it had been reported as stolen. He called it in as this morning's case was still fresh in the mind. He went a couple of roads up and called it in. The lads back at the station were on to it. They asked if any other vehicle could come and support the Mufty car. There was a squad car in Hillcrest Ave so they decided they would wait where they were and see what developed.

The Mufty driver kept an eye on the suspicious vehicle and when they moved off, he got on the radio to the squad car. Things happened in a few seconds. The suspicious vehicle screeched to a halt at the Dairy at the bottom of Otonga Road and the two robbers got out and entered the Dairy. The squaddie and the Mufty car drove up and boxed the stolen vehicle in. The driver of the stolen vehicle was out in a flash and legging it. Here's where it went wrong! The two police car drivers took off in pursuit of the driver! The lads in the two squad cars completely ignored the fact that there was an armed robbery going on inside the dairy!

He led them on a merry chase down Devon Street and it was at least two hundred yards before they caught him. Back at the Dairy in Otonga Road the two robbers had heard the commotion and got out of the shop where they went round the corner and legged it around the Chip shop on the roundabout and up Old Taupo Road towards the Golf Club. Only for a dark blue sedan to come screaming at them, pick them up and disappear over the brow of Old Taupo Road and away. One of the pursuers got a partial plate but that was it!

Never mind. We had one in custody and because they were involved in an armed robbery there was no chance, they would get bail. The Boss rang me immediately and we decided we would let the villain stew until the morning. I was in the middle of my studies, so I was happy to wait.

Tuesday

Why is it always hosing down in Rotorua? I got drenched running from the car park to the office and the Sarge was waiting for me with a decent coffee. The Boss and I had a coffee with the Sarge and discussed how we should best handle this case. Eventually we decided to go in and see what the villain said and perhaps see if he would co-operate.

The Villain was adamant. He would do his time. When we suggested he would be looking at seven years or more for an armed robbery using weapons, he blanched but said he would do it if it was needed.

We got nothing out of the offender even though we tried for the best part of an hour. The driver of the getaway vehicle, last seen speeding over the hill in Old Taupo Road, had reported his vehicle as missing, presumed stolen. It didn't help that he had inadvertently left his keys in the car because he had been 'keen to get in for a beer' at the Palace tavern. Obviously, he had gone in alone to the pub so we couldn't even finger one of his mates as a coconspirator. We all knew it was a phony story but without any other indications we knew we were on a hiding if we pursued the case.

The driver of the stolen car was remanded in custody and went up to Waikeria for evaluation. We had one of the thieves in custody which was a win for us.

The two DCs had a ring round the churches. There were two churches of interest. One was a mainstream church where the Vicar had tried to give a talk on Onanism to his bible class. Unfortunately none of his flock had any understanding of what the term meant. If he had used the more common vernacular, he might have made a bit more sense. As it was, the Boss merely puffed on about white middle class congregations not being in touch with the real world.

The second Church was one of the more fundamental churches. The Minister was away but his stand in had remembered the sermon very well. It was a very brave minister that used terms like 'onanism' and 'self-pleasuring'. And yes, he had been at the church when the sermon was delivered. Along with perhaps 150 other members of the congregation. At the Boss's request we arranged to go and see this guy and see what we could find.

At the minister's request we left it until the afternoon. That way he could also have a few members of his parish council available for us to speak with.

When we got to the church, we were met with a welcome committee of perhaps eight people. Obviously, this meeting had to start with a prayer for guidance. While everyone bowed their heads, the Boss and I looked at each other. This was not really our thing, and we were just a little uncomfortable.

The minister then asked us to ask any questions we felt like asking.

'Onanism.'

'The act of self-pleasuring. Many people do it, but it is not something that we should be doing to our bodies'.

'And spilling your seed onto the belly of a whore.'

'That is what the bible tells us.'

I reckon the Boss was about to go on one of his rants about the Church being out of date, so I took over.

'How does your church feel about gays? I know some churches openly accept the gays into their congregation.'

'Firstly, Detective Sergeant, we are not a congregation. We are a community who believe in God. Secondly, we are sad that some churches do accept the gay community into their ranks. But not this church! We believe that Homosexuality is a sin as described in the Bible. For us we would prefer them to accept the word in its entirety in preference to picking and choosing which bits we want to keep and which bits are inconvenient for our faith.

'When will your minister be returning?'

'He should be back to deliver his sermon on Sunday. He is away at the moment attending to his severely ill mother in Coromandel. Unless of course she is taken from us before that time.'

'I can't help but believe that one of your members has been spouting this.... What I should say is that there is a possibility that a member of your congregation of believers may have taken this message and used it to er... guide other people to the way you see as er.. right.'

'The way of the word is for an individual to follow as they see fit. Tell me detective sergeant. What is your way of preparing for the word of God?'

That is when the Boss took it over again. 'Thank you for sharing your wisdom in these matters. I don't think we will need to bother you again. Oh and I would appreciate your minister calling me on his return. It's only to tidy up some loose ends. Nothing really important but I would appreciate his call."

On our way back to the car the boss muttered "I don't care what the Sarge says. Religious nutters are what I am calling them."

On the way back to the station the Boss reckoned that if someone was following the words of this church, they could be up for anything, including a murder or two. He was unimpressed with their fervor.

When I got back, I had a message from Dave Powell. He had finished his studies and now he needed to apply for his exam. To do that he had to nominate a more senior officer to supervise his exam and for the exam to be sent to. I cheerfully agreed and he was happy that he could send away for his exam.

The Sarge and the Boss and I sat down for a meeting, and we discussed how we had got on this afternoon with the members of the church. The Boss declined to call them nutters in front of the sarge, but we all agreed that our murderer may indeed have come from this church. If nothing else, we had a fair idea that Janet's client was a member of their Congregation.

Wednesday

It was a slow day on Wednesday. The Boss was called by the Big Boss asking if we had anything to report to the papers. By that we assumed the Papers had been on to the Big Boss. The papers had gone on about how we should not let this person terrorize our citizens but had then completely forgotten about the practicalities of catching criminals. We had to be patient. The papers wanted everything solved like on the TV. One hour less the commercials was plenty of time on Telly. I think the Big Boss may have put them right on that score.

Also we got a letter from the Murderer. I was relieved because it partly told me that we only had one murderer to deal with. The letter had the single word 'Jezebel' written on it. That sent me scrambling for the dictionary, online, of course.

The Sarge beat me to it. "Jezebel. Wife of Ahab. Let me see." He grabbed the Office Bible from the Desk. Yes, there is a bible in every copshop so that if someone wants to swear on the bible, it's always available. He flicked through the Bible until he found the correct passage. "Married to Ahab. Blah, blah. Here it is. She set up a rival god and forced Ahab to choose. His God won so she was defeated. Seems she was the first feminist as her god was a woman. There's more but I reckon your lad is trying to say the victim was an unreliable person. Worshipped false gods and the like."

"So how does that help our case?" asked the Boss.

The Sarge thought about for a second before he answered. "Well it depends how you look at your life. Some people worship the God of wine or beer. Some worship sex. Some worship the Telly. What ever you reckon is most important in your life is what you worship. I don't know what your victim worshipped but whatever it was displeased the murderer."

The Boss opened his mouth a couple of times before saying, "Yeah, Thanks Sarge."

I went to see Janet, but it was only to see if we could get a better description of her client who had been all on to spill his seed etc. No I was only there for a quarter of an hour so don't think that harshly of me. I may have arranged a time for later that week but that is a separate issue and I'm sure there will be some line of enquiry for me to pursue. I was on my way out from Janet's, and I thought that maybe Derek could have a go with her phone. Maybe he could get a number out of Janet's phone. I went back in and asked Janet for her phone. She was happy provided I got it back to her so I took it into Derek to see if he could find anything.

Derek was one of those young guys whose fingers flickered over the keyboard way too fast for anyone to follow. He let out a couple of 'Ah's' and a couple of 'Hmm's' before giving the phone back to me.

"He's clever. Uses a VPN and then uses a VOIP. You'll never get his number out of that phone."

"Derek. Just supposing I knew half of what you are saying, can you explain that to me again."

"Sorry Sarge. A VPN is a virtual private network. It's what you use when you don't want someone to know where you are calling from.

Lets' say he has three VPN's going. He could make you think the call was from Bulgaria. If you tracked it down that call may be from the States. If you tracked that one down, you might find it originated in Russia. All of the while he may have been calling from across the street here in Rotorua. The sad thing is that you never really know when you have hit the last number. He may have one VPN, or he might have a dozen. Most of them are free now if you accept Ads. It's something they do to get free TV from the States, but they also use it for the phone being hidden."

" Yeah, er, thanks Derek. I'm sure I will know what the heck you are on about once I sit and think about it for a while. And what was the other thing you said?"

" VOIP. Voice over internet Protocol. Also he uses the internet to further evade your search. I'd say this guy is well skilled in technology. He is using over kill but if he wants to keep his number hidden from you, he will remain that way."

"Thanks Derek. And you learned all of that by pressing a few numbers on her phone."

"Call it a hobby of mine. If you wanted free phone calls for the rest of your natural, I could tell you how to do it but that is what we are cops for. Isn't it?"

"Much appreciated. Would this bloke have to do study or something to learn this lot?"

"No. it's not something you really learn about. It's the type of thing you pick up by being just a bit inquisitive. Either that or you go onto YouTube and sit through a few videos."

I thanked and left Derek and went to return the phone to Janet. She was grateful to get it back.

"And you have had no other thoughts about your client?"

"No. Oh he did say something odd. Something about onanism. I think that was what he said, I was too busy trying to get him to speed it up. He really gave me the creeps."

I was genuinely concerned for Janet's welfare. If this guy gave her the creeps as she said thenshould she be doing this kind of work. Janet reckoned it was all part of the fun. She never really knew from one time to the next if a new client was going to be 'a bit weird'. But then she said it was all a part of being available to these guys that was the fun part of it. And then she finished off by saying 'and besides. I do have some very nice regulars.' Yeah, that sort of shut me up for a while.

I went back to the office and as we all had not a lot to do, we sat and discussed the murder case until going home time.

Thursday

A nice and sunny day for a change. Even the Boss had a smile on his dial. There was nothing new to report on any of our cases, but it was a sunny day, so the Boss was happy. We sat over our coffee and discussed what else we could do to develop our case or cases. It was just after 9.00 and we were on our way back from the site of an assault, when we got the call about another armed robbery in progress at Turner drive. We did our best to get there quickly but it was all over when we arrived. There are probably 60 or 70 Dairies in town or at least in the outer suburbs. It's impossible to keep up with the patrols or even to work out which dairy might be hit next. There were a couple of Squaddies on the way there when we arrived there when we arrived, but we were the first o show up at the scene. The Boss had to park at the far end of the row. Mike and Derek had gone in their own car, and they parked at the near end of the parks available. The Boss and I were approaching from the right and Derek and Mike were approaching from the left. We were both about 5 yards from entering the business when a bloke in a dark tee shirt, sporting the 'Rolling Stones' logo walked out of the business holding a baseball bat and immediately fronted the two new DCs and made the not so polite enquiry. "And what the F***** do you pricks want, now!"

He swung up the Baseball bat ready to have a go at the two DCs. I was poised, ready to yell that we were the police. The Boss was more of a man of action. It was almost before I could realise what was happening that the Boss took a quick step forward. Grabbed the guy by the neck and had him roughly down on the ground all in less than a second. If I was that way inclined, I might have described the Boss's technique as a Miyoshi. As it was, one second the guy was ready to attack the two DCs and the next he was on the ground and rolled over onto his front and his arms were ready for the cuffs to go on! I might add that the Boss was not that gentle. Shouting to the two DCs, who were uncertain what to do next, the Boss shouted, 'get the cuffs on this prick'. By now the baseball bat was rolling on the ground, but importantly it was not near the assailant.

Then the Boss turned his attention to the guy on the ground. All of this was while he was kneeling on the middle of the guys back and holding him down. "And If I may be so bold as to use your vernacular, who the f*** are you?"

It had all happened so damn quickly, and I could vaguely hear a woman screaming in the background.

"Get that Bat in an evidence bag, Mike". And in that voice which meant he would tolerate no more nonsense "And like I said, and who the f*** are you?"

The guy on the ground was trying to speak and it was only when the blood stopped rushing through my ears, I heard him say. "If you listen to my Misses screaming you might know I am the owner of this bloody shop. Now get the hell off of me!"

In fairness to the Boss, the guy had come out swinging his bat around and had almost charged at the two DCs. In fairness to the bloke, the Boss might have been a bit rough on the takedown. But how was the Boss to know the guy was a relative innocent?

The Boss roughly picked up the bloke on the ground and got him to stand up. His nice tee shirt now had a big oil stain on the front of it from being unceremoniously dropped on the ground where the cars usually parked, when the Boss had swung into action. Mrs. Shop owner was still crying. So the Boss had to shut her up and get her to identify the Hubby. When she did, and the guy was busy telling the woman to shut up and identify him, the Boss told Mike to take the cuffs off.

There was a second or two when the Boss and the Shop owner looked at each other and might have reluctantly nodded that neither of them had handled the situation that well. The Owner was rubbing his wrists to get the circulation back and I stepped forward to try and calm things down.

Eventually the Owner said." If you're the Cops you'll probably want a brew. Come on inside then."

If you are offered a cup of tea or coffee, it's always been my habit to accept it. It means you will have at least another quarter of an hour to talk with the victim. Eventually we got the whole story, and we were well aided by the video camera footage. The owner was on an adrenaline high having just been robbed and when the two young lads, the two DCs, had tried to walk in the store the owner was still on an adrenaline high and had taken a swing at them at them thinking they were all part of the gang.

Sitting over a brew with the Boss we watched the footage. Mike and Derek had gone on a drive round to try and locate the stolen car the thieves usually used in a robbery of this type.

In rounding up the story, the two robbers had rushed into the store making a lot of noise. Then they had gone to the counter where the owner was stood. Shoving the shotgun in his general direction they had demanded he hand over all of the Cigs and Vapes. This owner was a bit more defiant. At his side was a baseball bat handy to his reach. He had grabbed the bat and swung in an arc. The leading robber, with the gun, was immediately flummoxed and he was also hit by the bat. He let off his shotgun which shattered a display case. The second robber grabbed his nearly unconscious mate and backed out of the door and into the waiting getaway car. We had arrived possibly twenty seconds or thirty seconds later along with the squad cars and you know what happened when we arrived. The Owner had taken one look at Mike and Derek and just assumed they were back for some more.

Mike and Derek returned at this point, so we sat and watched the Video footage again for their benefit. They had found the car in a side street off Pandora Ave and the print lads were going there first. By now the Boss and the owner were getting on very well. The Owner was an ex cockney, and they were used to having a good relationship with the local law.

The two new DC's were commenting on the video. When it got to the part where the shotgun went off Derek reckoned the guy was bloody lucky. The owner simply said, in that throwaway remark. "Yeah, but if fair f****d up my selection of Sherbert fizzes."

Perhaps it was the offhand way he made the comment that we all found absolutely hilarious.

I think it was Derek who first mentioned it. "Hey Sarge. If the owner took a swing at these lads there may be DNA evidence on the bat."

The Boss never missed a beat. He very nonchalantly replied, "That's why I got Mike to bag it as evidence. It could come in very handy if there is DNA."

The Boss and the owner exchanged a glance and a wink, and we were ready to leave the place.

Chapter 6

The Judge had not been impressed with the minister for the Sunday Service. As the new minister was away helping his sick mother, the old minister had stepped in to conduct the service and take the sermon. It was something about the 'Beatitudes and the sermon on the mount.' If the judge wanted to listen to waffle like that he would go to the local mainstream church! He wanted a sermon that preached hell fire and damnation. Well, something along those lines, anyway. Now he had heard that the new Ministers mother was near dying and he would have to put up with the old minister again for the next Sunday sermon. He was disappointed. His true calling was to help those girls who did not realise how they were tempting young men, and even older men, to abandon the way and have lustful thoughts. Was this a sign that the Judge should take a week off until the new minister returned. It was certainly something to pray about.

Friday

The Boss was excited. Today we should get the DNA results back on the Baseball bat the Dairy owner had swung. I was told we should the results back by mid-morning so everyone on the CIB team were waiting anxiously. Tim had an assault case from the previous night and Mike and Derek were sent to do the follow up. It was a domestic, but the wife had had enough, and she was determined to press charges this time. Even that tempting thought would not drag the Boss away from the Office.

At 11.00 the results came through and we were not surprised at the result. The local that had received a clobbering was one Tim O'Dowd. He was fairly well known to us. The Boss set about planning the pickup of Tim O'Dowd. The Sarge reminded us that Tim had a sawn off shotgun and suggested we use the Armed offenders squad team to help us. Reluctantly the Boss agreed which meant we had to organise things through the AOS team.

The AOS lads were something of a loose cannon in that they called the shots on any operation where they were involved. The head of the AOS team came down to visit us and it was decided that we should go in at 6.00 am on Saturday. Obviously, the Boss wanted to get the guy in a quicker manner, but the AOS team were in charge, so the Boss reluctantly agreed. The AOS Boss reckoned he would probably be in bed at that time and there was usually less of a chance of anyone in the neighborhood being up and about. It was all planned for the following morning. We would meet at 5.30am and go up to Mount View Drive in convoy. We would drive into Mount View Drive from either end and stop outside the house on either side. At a worst case scenario it would give us the protection of the vehicles as our cover if it all turned pear shaped. We would surround the property and call for the guy to surrender. We were told to expect a worst case scenario where the guy would not surrender and possibly make a run for it. Alternatively we may end up with a hostage situation where he took the family as his prisoner and then we would have a stand off until a hostage negotiator arrived. The Boss of the AOS team seemed to favour a short term resolution, but he did concede that the hostage negotiator did have some success on previous cases they had worked together. Nevertheless I was convinced that the Boss of the AOS team would prefer a quicker solution. I had my doubts about the AOS teams attitude, but I held my peace.

Then we got down to business as far as we were concerned.

"How many men will you have DI?"

"Four if not five." I figured that would include the Boss and I plus Derek and Mike and possibly Alan Kirk.

"You will be armed, obviously. Will you be taking arms from the weapons store, or would you prefer us to supply you with our weapons? As a weapon of choice we prefer the Steyr 45. An assault rifle and It's the one the Airforce use but it is a good tactical weapon and virtually no risk of a jam."

Now I realised just how seriously these guys took their weapons. They were comparing the choice of weapons as you or I might discuss the choice of which dessert to have.

The Boss replied. "We'll draw weapons from the Arms store. That will be a Glock 14 for each of us and we will hold back to allow your lads to do their thing."

"Right. We'll surround the house. Maybe we will need a couple of your lads to secure the perimeter. Once we are in position, I'll be in charge of the loudspeaker. We'll give him a chance to surrender and after that we'll hold a meeting at base 1 which will be outside number 57. Any questions?"

I couldn't help myself. I had to ask, "what is the likelihood of the guy surrendering first up?"

"Less than 34.8%. You know it hardly seems worthwhile getting the lads out and vested if the guy gives up without a struggle. But it does happen. Occasionally."

"Yeah Thanks. That's very comforting. "

"Don't worry DS. If it all turns pear shaped, our lads are in control and you lot will be pulled back to make a defensive barrier if the lad decides to do a Sundance."

The Boss asked. "What, may I ask, is a Sundance?"

"You know. At the end of the film where Butch and the Sundance kid make a run for it? Great scene, that."

The Boss seemed unimpressed. "Yeah, thanks for that."

The Boss of the AOS team left us to go and brief his squad. The Boss turned to me and the lads and said. "Those lads mean business. I'd have thought young Tim O'Dowd would have given himself up, but it looks like there is only a 34.8% chance of that happening." It was evident that the Boss was impressed with the serious nature in which the AOS took every situation.

At the new cop shop t he architect had installed a weapons testing range. The Boss suggested we might want to take a few magazines and fire them into the target cardboard cutouts. He would hate to let one of us freeze when it came time to pull the trigger. I did take the opportunity to have practice. I noticed Derek and Alan both sneaking off to have a shot as well. Tim Cross volunteered to go along with us as he already had his concealed carry license, but the boss suggested he cover the office and to expect a flood of calls at around 6.10am from the residents of Mount View Drive who had their sleep disturbed.

I took the chance to have a chat with Tim and asked how his part time job was going. He was disappointed. He was getting plenty of work that, so was not the problem. He had to cut himself down to a maximum of two days per week so he could sleep and be ready for his real job as a DC. His employer was asking him to consider going fulltime in the armed protection division as he was so skilled at it. It was generally acknowledged that by the time you were in your mid thirties you were getting a bit old for active duty in the armed protection team. Tim was twenty seven and he was being asked to head over to a team where he would have perhaps another 8 years of employment. He had thought about it and decided to stick with the Police force where he could anticipate a working life of at least twenty or thirty years. I did ask him had he guarded anyone important and he did give me a few names of people who had come down to Rotorua for a day. I will protect his confidences by not naming the people but it is a fact that if you see someone you recognize standing in the queue next to you at the Gondolas, you might consider taking a photo.

It was with some trepidation I went home and tried to relax for the evening. The Boss of the AOS team had disturbed my normal sleep patterns, so I watched the clock for most of the night until it got to

5.00am and I got up and took my shower. By 5.30 I was in the office and tooled up and wearing a bullet proof vest. I had to think to myself that this is the way of the world nowadays. In America they always come to work dressed like this. I reminded myself that this is one of the reasons I preferred to live in New Zealand where it is not a standard form of dress where you are constantly armed.

Saturday

I got in the Boss's car. His opening remark was to the effect. "Well if they shoot at this, it's over three years old. It will give me a chance to get a new motor." His mood did not necessarily reflect my mood.

It went like a well-oiled machine. We surrounded the property with our vehicles. Then we surrounded the property with the AOS team and moved in to gain the security screen so Tim O'Dowd could not slip past us. Then we waited for the guy on the loud hailer to do his thing. I was half hidden behind a cabbage tree and some kind of bush when the loud hailer went off.

First a piercing scream and then a loud authoritative voice.

"Timothy James O'Dowd. We have your home surrounded by members of the Rotorua Armed Offenders Squad. We ask you to show yourself at your front door with your hands in the air. You have twenty seconds to comply."

Twenty seconds is an awful long time when you are the one waiting for the front door to open. And somehow, I was directly in line with the front door! After a minute the guy on the loud hailer repeated his request and we waited again. I could sense the increased sense of readiness in the AOS team.

It was almost an anticlimax when the guys wife opened the door and threw out the sawn off shotgun. Then she appeared in the doorway and shouted, "He's still sick from the bashing he got from the bloke at the Dairy!"

This was something we had not anticipated. Evidently the lads from the AOS team were well prepared to storm the place in the event of the guy not fronting, but this was different.

I heard the Boss Shout. "Where is he?"

She replied, "He's still in bed. He wouldn't go to the Hospital. Reckons that would be the first place you buggers would look."

I could hear a conversation going on behind me between the Boss and the Boss of the AOS team.

My Boss had his way. He usually does!

While I was waiting for things to be decided behind me. I was looking at my position. I had on my bullet proof vest, and I was holding my Glock in the crouched position. It's odd how you remember things at this point. I had made a conscious decision to leave my Jacket in the Boss's car, as If I was shot at I wouldn't want a hole in my jacket as it was fairly new. I remembered my firearms instructor being disappointed with me for curling my left forefinger around the trigger guard. And he corrected my position and told me to always have the left forefinger aiming towards where you want to shoot. I consciously extended my forefinger to the general direction I would be shooting in, if I ever managed to shoot the Glock.

The Boss shouted." I want you and any kids to come out with your hands up and walk towards my voice."

The woman disappeared and then reappeared within a minute. Her and a couple of kids walked out towards the Boss's car. There was a hurried conference between the Boss and the AOS team Boss and the lady. Then the guy on the loudhailer did his thing again. "Timothy James O'Dowd. If you do not come out, we will come inside the house and take you out in handcuffs. My team is well armed. If you show any signs of resisting arrest we will shoot you. Do you understand?"

The Woman was trying to tell the AOS team boss that her hubby was crook as, and in no condition to put up a fight. The AOS team boss was rightfully playing it with care.

After a minute there was some secret sign made and half a dozen of the AOS team entered the house with Weapons off the safety position and ready for action.

We waited for a minute and then we saw the unit leader of the AOS team come out and give a thumbs up. They had found Tim O'Dowd virtually unconscious on his bed with a huge bruise on his forehead. It was like a signal going off. Everyone on our side relaxed. The Boss didn't exactly rush in but he did go in and was directed to Tim's Bedroom. He was out in a couple of seconds and on the phone for an ambulance. Tim required urgent medical attention.

For myself I found it difficult to actually come down from the high. Yes, I was not happy to be in that position, but it was one of the things I joined the Police force for. To be a part of this adrenaline rush. I decided that I was probably a bit old for this much adrenaline. I went over to the Boss, and he was angry that Tim had come home when he needed medical attention. He should have gone straight to the A&E dept at the Hospital.

Oh, and there was one thing I took note of while we were surrounding the house. The AOS Boss had a long lead from the microphone to the actual loudhailer. Maybe twenty meters long. And he used the full length of the wire to make sure the loudhailer was twenty yards away from him. When I asked afterwards about it, he reckoned that it was the voice of experience coming in to play. The first shot is always aimed at the bloke on the loudhailer. Using a twenty meter cable ensured that the shot would not come at himself or any other member of the team. I thought that was quite clever. He reckoned it was the years of experience.

The Ambulance arrived and made him stable enough to go to the hospital. The Boss of the AOS team was walking around and telling his men to stand down. Having been a part of that scenario I could understand the need to tell his men it was all over. I was still walking around and fully aware I had a loaded Glock 14 on my hip. What would I have done if I needed to pull the trigger. I dunno. I assume basic training would have kicked in and I would have responded appropriately. If I have to say one thing, though. I fully appreciate the training these AOS lads go through and knowing they might be in a live firing situation when they get the call. I was glad I was not one of them!

The Boss arranged for a Squaddie to stand guard outside the Prisoners room at the Hospital. We later learned that Tim had suffered a fractured skull as part of the Dairy owner swinging the bat around. Along with the fractured skull he had a brain bleed. They operated on him immediately and did something with the brain bleed. Cauterized it or something like that. Then they fixed his broken skull while he was still under his anesthetic.

Once he was under intensive care at the hospital it was conveyed to us that he was in no immediate danger, and we should be able to interview him within a couple of days. Alan Kirk was in that Saturday. He logged in 14 calls complaining about the noise at 6.00 AM And among the calls was one guy that reckoned we should have waited until at least 9.00 before shutting off the street etc. When I had a chance to think about it all, I was most upset for the two young kids who were involved. For me, I always feel sad when the dad getting arrested is just a part of growing up. What message is that sending?

I settled down for the rest of the day although it took me a while to come down from the high. Part of me realised what a thankless job we were doing and part of me realised what a valuable job we were doing in keeping the streets relatively safe.

Sunday

I slept well last night. Perhaps it was because of the disturbed sleep I had gone through the previous night. I woke up to a glorious almost spring day. Considering it was the middle of winter I must say I was enjoying the pleasant day.

The Sarge and the Boss were already on the tee when I arrived which meant I had to forgo my usual ten minutes of practice on the putting green.

Can I say I was on fire! I birdied two holes on the front nine. Yes, I admit I was perhaps a bit lucky and I was close to another couple of birdies on the back nine. A three over on the17th, thanks to a trip into the trees down the left hand side, put me in my place for the day but I was still very pleased overall.

At the end of the round I had shot a 95 and none of us had ever broken the hundred mark. I did know I would pay for it for the next few weeks as my handicap would drop markedly. But as both the Sarge shot 100 and the Boss shot a 101 we were all fairly pleased with our efforts. The Sarge and the Boss both reminded me to make sure I put my scorecard in to the box before we went upstairs and the Boss bought us a beer.

Monday

Another glorious day and today we would be interviewing Tim O'Dowd.

Even the Boss was in a good mood when he walked into the office. Also on my desk was an envelope with the Senior Constables exam for Dave Powell. I rang David and we arranged to do the exam the following afternoon starting at 1.00.

At 9.00 the Boss rang the hospital and at 10.00 we were up at the hospital and ready to interview Tim.

We had a word with the Nurse, and she said Tim was fine but if he started to tire, we were to leave him alone and try again later.

It all had to be formal and the Squaddie on door duty listened in to make sure we were doing it correctly.

Tim started to argue with us straight away. Reckoned he might have just gone into the dairy for Chewing gum.

When he had finished protesting his innocence the boss asked him if it was normal for Tim and His mate to enter a shop with a sawn off shotgun and wearing a mask that covered each of their faces when you are only going in for Chewing gum. It was laughable that he was arguing with his skull covered in bandages but that is what you get with modern crims. They know their rights, even if they have not quite worked them all out in a logical manner.

He was caught dead to rights and then he asked us what he could expect from the courts.

The boss replied. "At least 7 to 10 years. You were armed with a shotgun and waving it around and terrifying the other customers. Not looking good for you, Tim. Of course we could always tell the court that you co-operated and gave us the names of your associates. But I would want the name of your mate and also the lad who was driving the getaway car.

I added. "And let's not forget the name of your back up driver. We'd want his name as well."

I was keen to try and pin all of the armed robberies on this guy, but he bristled when I said that. He would admit to four robberies, but another gang had done the other three and he would not name that gang either.

Tim thought for just a second and then said, "Nah. I can't give you three names. I'll take this on the chin. I might be out in five if I behave myself."

And that was it. He would persistently refuse to give us any names and he kept with that right through his trial. The Nurse reckoned he would be there for observations for the next couple of days and then it was up to us to deal with him. We tried him a couple of different ways, but he was adamant. The Boss and I left to go back to the station when we got the call about another armed Robbery taking place.

Out towards the Airport around Pohutukawa Drive there was a Dairy on the Main road being robbed. We knew we would be late, but we set off anyway. Mark and Derek were already on the way there.

Hopefully this time they would hold up their ID warrants before entering the shop.

By the time we got there the two DC's had everything covered so the Boss and I went for a drive to see if we could see the usual stolen vehicle left abandoned by the Robbers. We found the vehicle in a layby on the Whakatane Highway. It was an older vehicle, a Ute type of thing, with a stick shift or manual gearbox. As long as it was reliable, I suppose it didn't matter to the robbers. We knew that Tim O'Dowd's gang were methodical in their thefts. We always had the hope that there would be a fingerprint or DNA sample to work with, but we had been unsuccessful so far.

We sent the Fingerprint lads to do the stolen car first and then we went back to the scene of the crime. We had a 'wannabe' hero in the shop. Says he might have got out his baseball bat and had a swing at them, but his Missus was in the shop along with a couple of customers, so he decided not to take on the Robbers. Mike had already told him that was the smart thing, and he was pleased that he did not have a go and could he describe the robbers. His description of the robbers was fairly poor. The usual average height and average build etc. Not a lot for us to go on. Given that this gentleman, the Owner, was of Asian descent and about five foot high, I would have expected a bit more of him but that was what we got out of him.

It was only when we got back to the station, and we got the feedback from the Fingerprint lads that Derek checked the Prints and found.

We had a match!

I can only assume that the Robber who was the driver had removed his glove to get a better feel of the gear stick and they had forgotten to wipe the gear stick although they had remembered to wipe clean the steering wheel. We had a clear thumb print on the gear lever. To make matters even better, we also had the guys prints on our database.

Matthew Dimitri Dillon. A known felon. Used to driving fast cars as he had seven speeding tickets plus unlicensed driving on his rap sheet. Along with a couple of stints inside for GBH and an unrelated Burglary. Dimitri is an odd name. even for a middle name. I assumed he would have got some stick for that name in school.

We were fairly certain that Matt Dillon did not have a gun but we decided to get the AOS team out again. Maybe it was for their benefit or maybe it was the sight of the sawn off shotgun being casually tossed out onto the lawn on last Saturday. We did know someone in the group carried a revolver with them, so it was best not to take any chances.

The AOS team Boss came down and had another word with us. The usual thing How many men would we be deploying, and would we be armed and did they want us to supply their weapons. The Usual type of thing.

It was all set down for the Tuesday Morning. Meet at 5.30 and draw weapons. Then go in convoy to the street. Approach from both ends of the street and then secure the perimeter, and then the Boss of the AOS team would do his thing on the loud hailer.

It was close to 5.00 when I got a call from the Police psychologist, Colin Handley. He had been meaning to make contact but he had been involved with a shooting threat to one on the MP's which had been taking his attention. He called me to see how his profiling went with the arson/weed killer offender.

We had a good chat and he was pretty spot on with his assessment.

Single or married with a loveless marriage. Our guy was married but the wife had been fairly unemotional when we spoke to her. So yes it seemed like a loveless marriage.

Below average height. If average height was around 1.75 meters this guy would have maxed out at perhaps 1,68 meters tall so he did have the little guy mentality.

The world owed him. He had an argument with the picture framer about something that was obviously his own fault.

He suggested I go back to the guy and hit him with the lack of publicity at his early efforts with the weed killer. If he could admit to that he would likely admit to all of the weedkiller and the arson charges to make sure he got full credit for his crimes.

I said I would let the Psychologist know if I had any success. Right know I had other things on my plate.

Tuesday

Surprisingly I slept well that night. I woke at 5.00 and had my shower and was into the weapons room by 5.30. I was now getting nervous, but I had a good night's sleep, so I was better prepared. We left the station in convoy and went up to Hillcrest Ave. Going in from both ends we blocked the road off and this time there were people moving around and going to work etc. They had to amend their route to work but we had our own problem to deal with and the Boss told me to tell them sod off if they were becoming aggro. I reckon that is easier said than done when you are dealing a member of the public at six AM.

We secured the perimeter of the house. This time I was at the rear of the property and covering a window. I felt safer but I was still curling my finger around the trigger guard. I straightened my finger and waited for the loud hailer.

When it finally happened it shook me for a moment until I realised what we were here for.

"Matthew Dimitri Dillon. This is the Rotorua AOS team, and we are armed. Please show yourself at the front door of your property with your hands up. You have twenty seconds to comply."

It wasn't my imagination. I definitely saw someone look out of the window. He waved at me to acknowledge he had seen me. I was on full sensory alert. 'Please don't let the bastard come through my window'.

The occupant disappeared. I later discovered that he went around the house looking for avenues of escape. When he decided that all avenues of escape were blocked off he disappeared from view and went quiet.

After a minute the guy on the loudhailer repeated his request and silence descended on the street.

The Boss relayed all of the happenings to us later.

The Boss and the Boss of the AOS team had a conference.

"Do we go in or do we wait for a hostage negotiator?" Asked the Boss of the AOS team.

The Boss was very succinct in his reply. "How the hell should I know?"

"If you are happy for me to take charge, please stand back and give me room to operate." That was from the Boss of the AOS team.

Things happened quickly from that point. The AOS team were about to enter the property which involved half of them withdrawing strategically, to form up in a new and more attacking strategy.

Everything was centered on an assault on the front door with the rest of us all around to prevent any other egress by the Villain. I was hunkering down and preparing myself for when the attack happened. And then...anticlimax!

The Villain opened his front door and tossed a revolver onto the lawn. With this development the AOS team Boss got back on the loud hailer. "Walk out of your door and along the concrete path until I tell you to stop."

There was a natural slope up to the front door, so the concrete path followed the house and then down to the driveway. The AOS team were well hidden at the edge of the section.

Matt did as requested. At a point the Boss of the AOS team asked him to kneel and then lie face down. Two officers approached the villain. One holding the Steyr rifle pointed at the guy and the other with handcuffs. It was all over in a few seconds. The guy was cuffed and stuffed into a police van and we were told to stand down and holster our weapons. For me I was still on the high. I could imagine how the AOS team lads felt when they had a fairly tame outcome. I got to escort the prisoner back to the cells. I was first relieved of my gun. That was for the best, I thought to myself. I was happy to be relieved of its presence. Somehow, I felt very responsible when I was armed.

We got Matt back to the Station, and he was trying to find out what we had caught him for. I remained quiet during the drive to the station. I had other things on my mind. If he had come at me out of the window, would I have had the nerve to use the weapon? Probably, I would have but there is always that doubt when you are tested.

We left Matt alone for an hour while we went upstairs to the café and had our breakfast. I noticed the AOS team were tucking in. I did not question their bravery in being out in that situation and they deserved every cent they got for the extra duty allowance.

At 8.00 we went down to the holding cells and got the prisoner to the interview room. The sarge was in the adjacent room as he wanted to see how we went along with Mike and Derek. Alan was back in the CIB room. I'd guess that even the Sarge had given up on Alan being an asset to our team by now.

The Boss started with. "Right, Matt. We already have Tim and his gang and now we have you. Are you going to save yourself a few years inside by telling us the names of your mates?"

Matt was quite calm. He thought about the Boss's opening remark and then said. "Detective Inspector, I don't reckon you have Tims gang at all. You might have Tim O'Dowd, but I don't reckon he would tell on his mates. If you will tell me who you have then I might consider turning Queens Evidence."

I couldn't help myself, "It's Kings Evidence. We have a king now!"

Matt turned and looked at me. "King or queen. I don't care. Tell me who you have?"

The Boss's bluff had been called and he knew it.

"I'm not at liberty to tell you about other prisoners on remand."

"Because you don't have anyone other than Tim. And that's because he got a belt from the owner. What have you got me for? Stolen car and that's it."

The Boss was pleased to be able to elaborate on Matt's involvement. "Well we will get you for stealing a car. It doesn't matter if it's a piece of crap, it's still worth time, inside. Then we have you as part of an armed gang robbing a dairy and stealing, I'd reckon about ten grands worth of smokes. That has to be worth between 7 and ten years, wouldn't you say Detective Sergeant?"

"Possibly even more if we can prove a conspiracy to commit the armed robbery. Then there's premeditation in nicking the motor for the express purpose of robbing a dairy. Don't forget about the other three Dairies Matt was a part of robbing. I can see a decent jury going as far as twelve years if the Crown prosecutor is on the form he has been for his last few trials. And don't forget Matt seemed to be hanging onto the revolver. I'd reckon we are up for at least 12 years."

Matt was tight lipped but he was not about to rat on his mates so we charged him with the charges we could and left him to think about things. On the way back to the office the Boss reckoned we would struggle to get anything out of Tim or Matt. They would probably just do the time and see it as a badge of being dishonest. There was a good chance that disturbing the Gangs would see them put an end to the Dairies robberies.

When we got back to the CIB room Alan had already had a number of complaints about the noise at 6.00 by the armed offenders squad. The Boss's reply was unprintable, so I won't bother with it.

It was just after 9.00 and the Boss and I and Mike and Derek had already put in what seemed like a full day when the Boss's phone rang. It was the Big Boss demanding a meeting with everyone on the CIB and right now!

As we wandered up to the Big Boss's office, My Boss wondered what would be getting up the big Boss's knickers.

We were soon to be advised of the situation.

The Boss had a call from the local Rag and also one from the Nationals. It seems like it was a slow news day, so they were doing a story on Rotorua's serial killer. As a courtesy they had asked the local Police chief to advise on any progress they had made. There was also a not so subtle comment about the recent article on Rotorua Police getting tough on Crime. The Boss wanted everyone to focus on what he should tell the papers.

The Boss's initial reaction that it was not his problem was sharply overridden by the CI. It made Rotorua look bad. It made the police force look bad. And what had we done to catch the offender. Etc.

I was keeping well under the radar and sitting on the edge of the people gathered when the Big Boss noticed me. "You have a DS and half a dozen DC and a sergeant babysitting you. Surely, we can come up with something better than 'enquiries are being made."

It seems that the Boss had not yet made his report about this morning's incident, yet. I'm going to say he was perhaps still on the same high from this morning. However, at this point the general conversation quickly deteriorated into an argument between the Big Boss and My Boss. After a few seconds The Big Boss called the meeting over and he would continue discussions with the Detective Inspector once the rest of us had left. There was an orderly leaving of the Big Boss's office that was akin to fighting your way onto the train at the rush hour. We left the two Inspectors to discuss the situation while we convened back in our office.

The Boss emerged from the meeting around a half hour later with the announcement that we would be setting up a special task force to pursue the Murderer. I did ask who was on the special task force and the Boss said, "You lot."

When I asked who would be covering all of the other crimes going on in Rotorua, the Boss replied "You lot!"

With that he went into his office and shut the door. He had to write something about the progress in our cases over the last few weeks. He was going to struggle to say 'sod all' in a way that would sound as if we had done something.

Chapter7

The Judge had sat and suffered through the Old Ministers preaching on the Sunday Service. His sermon had centered around the story of the Five loaves and seven fishes with which Jesus had fed the five thousand.

Hopefully the new minister will be back for next week's service. It was an odd feeling for the judge to be passive. He thought he had a mission to teach these young girls how to behave and better comport themselves to be loyal wives to God fearing men. Yet he had been forced to listen to how the Lord had fed a crowd of five thousand with the sheer goodwill of the rest of the crowd members. And why had none of the crowd, or just a few of the crowd had thought ahead to bring food along. Yes, he had been passive for the last few days. Was it a sign that he was supposed to be resting in readiness for his mission?

The sarge had listened to the Boss's comments and he waited for the Boss to disappear into his office before he came and joined us.

Mike and Derek and I sat down with the Sarge, and we discussed our future in terms of catching this murderer.

We had gone through the suggestions on the whiteboard again just last night. Mike and Derek were looking to me for their inspiration. I had nothing to really add. I was still on a high about getting the Armed Robberies tidied up.

When the conversation started to peter out, the sarge voiced his opinion. "Forget about the Murderer. He will make a mistake and you will get him. They always do. Secondly. I reckon you might be making a big mistake with the armed Robberies. Who's to say they won't join forces and keep on with them? You already know that Tim and this lad Matt know each other. They have lost a driver for the getaway vehicle and Tim's mob have lost the brains of the outfit. Don't be surprised if a new gang takes on a few more dairies. And by a new gang, I mean the old ones will reform."

I looked at the Sarge and thought he was probably right.

The Sarge continued. "I don't know what you can do or where you can park to keep up with this mob but I reckon you might not have heard the last of this gang. What you lot have to do is to be better prepared to respond to an armed Robbery a bit quicker."

I presented myself to one of the conference rooms at 12.45 and Dave Powell came in at just before 1.00. I sat down and read the papers and did a crossword and a sudoku while Dave did his papers for the Senior constable exam. I did some reading and then some work on my laptop. I was interested that Dave would be one of the youngest Senior constables on the force. He was only 32 and had joined the force at 18. Said he always wanted to be a copper and his studies at school were always in that general direction.

Dave was finished ahead of time, and I did my officiating duties and sealed the papers in the envelope provided. At 5.00 I took Dave up for a beer to the Police Pub. He was saying how he would miss Rotorua. It seems he had got quite fond of working with the Boss and I. He said we were always available if he had a question. I told him that now he had passed his Senior Constable exam, hopefully, he would be the one the juniors would ask for help. He said he was looking forward to it. We finished our beer, and I went home.

Things got very quiet for a few days. Yes, there were the usual Crimes of GBH and assault and domestic violence, but they were being handled by the night crew of Tim or Dave. Occasionally Alan would get a call, but he seemed to pass it on to the weekday crew to tidy things up. Importantly we had no new murders or sexual assaults and also, we had no new cases of armed robbery to deal with.

I think the Papers may have taken a little credit for the lull, although I can't see why?

Wednesday

It might have been on Wednesday around 10.00AM when we got a call about an armed robbery in progress in Ngongotaha. Again it was a dairy although a different dairy from the time before. Obviously, we were not going to get there in time to do any good so the four of us went out in two cars and assessed the damage. We assumed it was new gang or at least a mix up of the old gangs.

When we looked at the video footage it made us laugh. The two robbers had entered the dairy and for no explicable reason the shotgun had gone off which blasted a hole a foot or so across into the unmarked case which held the cigarettes. We couldn't hear what the robbers were saying as the video had no sound, but everyone on the shop froze for a second. The back up robber said something to the main robber. Then the main robber, the one with the gun, told the attendant to fill up the backpack with cigs and vapes. As he had just shot up the cigarette cabinet, the attendant filled up the backpack with the cigs that were suffering the most from having a shotgun blasted into them. It may have been a minute later that the second robber told him to forget it and grabbed the backpack and the second robber and they backed out of the shop and went to the waiting car and drove off.

It was like one of those early comedy films without the sound and it was a right cock-up! On closer examination of the scene I noticed that the attendants arm was showing spots of blood. When I pointed this out to the guy, we realised that the Attendant had worn the extreme edge of the shotgun going off. He only had a couple of pellets in his arm. But it was enough that he would forever be known as the guy who stood up to the Armed robbers.

I called for an ambulance to attend and then we went through the footage again. By this time Mike and Derek had returned. They had found the stolen car in Hood Street and the print lads were going there first to check it out. This time they were way more optimistic of getting a print to work with. It was thanks to their efforts that we had caught Matt Dillon.

We were still hoping the Fingerprint lads would find something at the shop, but we already noticed that the Gang had not removed their gloves at any point. The Ambulance arrived to much cheering from the locals and the attendant was ushered into the ambulance to treat his wounds. The Attendant was very much the hero of the day for his efforts. For me he had done nothing other than be in the way of the accidental shotgun blast but if the locals wanted a hero they had this attendant.

We left the crime scene tape up with a squaddie on guard. We had the video footage which we took back to the office. On the way back we discussed the case and how we would probably be mauled in the local papers for our inability to stop these gangs.

When we got back to the Station Derek set up the Video and we all watched it again. The Sarge did have a chuckle, but he reckoned it might even make the Telly if it was a slow news day.

Within the hour we had the Big Boss on our backs looking for a quote for the papers. They had been on to him and enquiring as to the state of our investigation. Here's where the papers get you. If they come out all aggressive you automatically go on the defensive. If they come at you considerably you tend to answer them with a bit more warmth and friendliness. That way they can use nearly anything you say and add a twist to it. Obviously, it's all in the quest to be good journalists. Whatever!

By midafternoon we had the TV cameras set up outside the new Station and the Big Boss and my Boss were being interviewed. My Boss was there under the strict instructions of the Big Boss. He wanted someone else to share this very penetrating spotlight.

I have to say I watched them both being interviewed and what the media actually said was astounding. I was amazed at how they could bend the nuance of everything the Boss and the Big Boss said.

However, we had a meeting in the Bull pen to discuss the latest developments. The Bull pen was what we had called the general meeting space in our office. It's real name was the 'Bullshit pen' but no one needs to know that.

We had a meeting after which the Boss made a few decisions. Mike and I were to go over to Waikeria to reinterview Tim O'Dowd and Matt Dillon, separately. Our role was to show them the video footage of the latest robbery. We were given pretty much free range to try and get one of these lads to talk. We could use the amateurishness of the robbery, the fact that they had reformed withing a few days so what use was the loyalty of the lads already banged up inside. Someone was going to get murdered with an accidental discharge of a weapon. Would they want that on their conscience? Would they like being an accessory to murder if they knew the names and withheld them? Okay this was pushing it a bit, but the Boss told us to try anything.

I arranged to interview the Waikeria lads at 10.00 and 11.00 the following day. That afternoon I went to see Tiff for an hour. We had a lot to er... talk about.

Thursday

In at my usual time and the Sarge was ready to hand me my coffee. I have to say that the sarge was getting to be a dab hand at this coffee making. And I was getting it at less than a Dollar a cup. Within a few months I would be well ahead of paying Café prices!

At 8.30 Mike and I set off for Waikeria. The Boss suggested I take Mike and he would then be familiar with the procedure at Waikeria.

At 10.00 we were sat down with Tim O'Dowd. When he looked at the Video footage he couldn't help but have a laugh. His initial comment was ""F****** amateurs."

Try as I might I still could not get Tim to give us any names. His attitude was that 'unless they get better at it, and pretty damn soon, You lads will have them in custody, soon.'

Try as I might I could not get him to talk about this gang. He did admit that they looked a bit like one of his lads but that was all he would say.

When I suggested he might be up for an accomplice to a murder if they ever accidentally killed some poor shop owner, he called my bluff." Am I right in thinking you're stretching it a bit with that one?"

We had a good half hour to kill so Mike and I went up to the Cafeteria and had a coffee. Definitely not as good as the Sarge's but still passable. We discussed how we should handle Matt Dillon. Mike had a couple of suggestions, so I let him take the lead with Matt.

Again, we drew a blank. Matt did agree these robbers were acting too dangerously, but the best we could get out of him was that he would have a word with someone and give them a few clues as to how to behave in that situation.

All in all it was a bit of a waste of our time.

We also had some time with the Arson guy who was on remand at Waikeria. Going with the psychologists advice I hit him up about not getting all of the publicity for his crimes. At first I thought the guy wasn't going to talk, but once he started he was a hard man to shut up. Maybe it was because he had been locked up for a few days. Whatever, he was now way more talkative. Yes, he deserved way more credit for his activities. Did we know what they were teaching in the schools now. It was all about the treaty and how we should be giving the Māori's a head start before our kids even got a chance. I was already to charge him with everything when Mike shut me up. This guy was talking himself into a decent sentence if I would let him continue to hang himself. He confessed to all of the crimes over the next half hour. As best as I could imagine it all came down to a bit of small man's syndrome and the his dissatisfaction with the Māori tribes being given such a head start, in his opinion. Then we he started spreading the dislike around. He let on that in the area he lived in, there was a local Sikh who had bought the dairy. So now Sikh's and them Hindus were getting some of the blame as well. Then it was the Muslim's who got a part of the blame because they were coming over here and not staying to fight for their homeland. At one point even the Poms were getting the blame because they were taking down the crosses in their church to make the Muslim brothers and sisters feel welcome. The last I heard, that was back in England but I was listening to this guy get all worked up and digging himself deeper into the mess. I was getting a bit bored with all the ill feeling I was getting and we had already charged him with all six offences, so Mike and I spent a half hour in the warder's break room writing down everything we could remember from our chat with the arsonist. By the end of a half hour we had more than enough evidence to charge him with everything. I don't know, maybe his time inside had made him further add to the injustices he felt he had received. Whatever, we had more than enough to add a load of things to the evidence log against him.

We got back to the Station in Rotorua at around 2.00. The Boss had been busy and had reworked the whiteboard along with Derek. Other than the words 'New Gang' at the top there didn't seem to be anything more than I had before. Oh, and there was the word 'Amateur' across the bottom.

Also the Boss had grabbed another Whiteboard from somewhere. Together with Derek and the Sarge they had also spent time brainstorming the murders. I was in something of a funk having had a less than successful time with my trip to Waikeria with the ram-raiders. I was still pleased we'd got the arsonist to cop for everything he had done. But seeing the ideas the Boss and Derek and the Sarge had for the murder case as well didn't do me that much good. We'd only taken the Arson lad as an extra and it had paid off for us. I still had to come up with something for the murders and the rapes.

After we had lunch the Boss grabbed the lot of us and called a meeting in the Bull pen. He waited until we were all sat down and then said, "Forget what the local rag is saying. We have a Killer on our hands who we reckon is a religious fanatic. Derek reckons he is a religious nutter, but the Sarge reckons we have to be polite. Whatever you call him he needs to be found! And we also have a gang or a couple of gangs turning over dairies for fags and vapes. At times like this we tend to get hard on ourselves. Let me tell you this. Neither the Killer nor the Armed gangs have given us a clue as to who they are. As soon as they do, we'll have them! Your job is to get out there and not miss any clue they might leave us and then work the hell out of that clue. Forget the Papers and forget what the Boss upstairs is saying in the press. I have confidence in you lads to get these Buggers. Remember, we only want one clue, and we have someone doing time! Now I've got to go and see the Boss for my weekly grilling about what we aren't doing down here. But I reckon it won't do you any harm to have a look at these boards Derek and I have set up. Maybe you have something to add. Maybe you reckon we are looking in the wrong direction? I don't care what it is you are thinking. Get it down on the Whiteboard. DS it's over to you."

With that he went upstairs to see the Big Boss. When I really looked at the two whiteboards Derek and the Boss had indeed reworked some of our ideas. With the general chitchat we came up with a few new items to think about and I asked everyone to consult with their CI's to see if we could get something from hearsay.

Chapter 8

The Judge had been quite passive with the new minister not being in charge of the Sunday service. It goes without saying that he had noticed so many loose women who were flaunting their bodies for everyone to gaze at. Most of them seemed to be pleased with the attention they were getting but for the most part he could tell that most men were only taking a sideways glance at what was on offer. But taking a sideways glance they were and that was a sin. The Sin was obviously having lustful thoughts. He had even gotten into the habit of following a young girl home. He told himself it was purely for the practice of following a young girl and he was certainly not capable of having lustful thoughts himself. He thought about it and decided it was time to visit a whore again. Deep inside he had been having lustful thoughts about some of the young girls he was following, and he was aware that it was a sin of his own Commission. If he visited a whore perhaps the lustful thoughts would go away. Then again, he was not surprised that the girls he had been following had driven him to sinful thoughts with the way they dressed. Oh how he needed the new minister back for some guidance..

If his mission was to stop these brazen girls, he might as well keep in his practice. He would only know his true mission when the new minister returned on Sunday. If the Minister spoke of the end times or about brazen hussies he would know he had a role to play. His life was not easy but as they say, it's hard for a man to pass through the eye of a needle. He was that man if that is what the minister spoke about.

<u>Friday</u>

I think I was feeling positive. It was a nice sunny Winters Day and the sarge was making the coffee when I walked into the Office.

I'd disappeared five minutes early the previous day. Maybe I had had enough to the CIB world for one day. I did spend a couple of hours on my senior sergeants exam study, so I suppose it cancelled out.

The Sarge reckoned the Boss had come down from the Big Boss's office in a fairly poor temper. The Big Boss had been fairly pleasant for most of the interview and my Boss was waiting for the hammer to fall on him. In a very roundabout way, it did!

The Big Boss had heard about the Boss and I and the sarge going out for a weekly round of Golf. He wondered whether it was ok to join us for a round!

The Big Boss played off a handicap of eighteen strokes. The three of us were playing off the low thirties. Well I had dropped down to 29 because of my recent good game. And he was happy to play at Springfield, our local course, and he was happy to play on a Sunday. The Boss could not really refuse so it was all teed up for our usual time at 11.00 on the Sunday.

It's hard to know how to play a game like this. Do you let the Boss win and congratulate him on his victory? Or do you try your damn hardest to beat the bugger and have crowing rights for the next few months. The Boss decided for all of us. Whoever was on the Big Boss's side could play their best but whoever was not on the Big Boss's side had better be prepared to play well!

It was later that night, around 11.30, when I got the call from Tim, who was covering the evening shift. "Gidday Boss. We might have another of your rape cases going on. Do you want to be involved?"

Almost as soon as the phone rang I had swung my legs out of bed and I noticed it was quite cold! I knew I couldn't pass on this one so I asked where it was and said I would meet him up there. I got the address as Luke Place up in Kawaha Point. There was a bridge across the stream that cut through to Barnard Road. Our perpetrator had followed the girl down the walkway and attacked her as she crossed the bridge.

When I drove up to the scene of the attack I could see it was well covered by bushes and the like. A good place for an attack if there was such a thing.

The girl was being attended to in the ambulance and the K9 unit were trying to track the offender in Barnard Road. I always feel sorry for the girls in a sexual assault. Some guy attacks a girl because they feel a bit horny. Tim was interviewing the girl in the Ambulance and afterwards he spoke with me. "I'm not sure if this is our guy. Yes he raped her and there is no DNA other than going through her pubic hair to see if there is any stray hair down there. This guy said nothing about being saved by god or anything like that. Your last case, you reckoned he was all over about god's forgiveness. I hate to say it, but I don't reckon this is our religious idiot."

Tim and I discussed the case for a couple of minutes. By which time the K9 unit had drawn a blank in Barnard road. I made arrangements to see Tim in the CIB room at 4.00 when he clocked in. He said he would have his report in to my computer when I got to work. Tim reminded me I would not be in until Monday. Tim went off to the hospital to get any DNA samples we could. I went back to my unit and returned to my bed. Another rapist? Just what I needed!

Sunday

We turned up at our usual time for the game on Sunday. Nice day but a little bit cloudy. Maybe we would get rain later in the round.

Can I say, I was still playing like a champ!

It was decided that the Sarge and the Big Boss would play together as they were still part of the Uniform branch. The Boss, and I would play together as we were the lads in Civvies.

I have to say that the Big Boss looked the part. He had on a very nice Jumper, obviously a Pringle design which is what all of the top golfers wear if they are keen to be a fashion icon. Plus he had a bag full of Calloway irons and metal woods.

The rest of us looked like poor cousins. We had all bought a secondhand set from the local pro.

The Big Boss went first. He did his practice swing and then addressed the ball. There must be some rule in golf that says how long you have to take your shot and the Big Boss used every second. Mind you his swing was straight down the middle. The Big Boss had suggested we play a four ball, whatever that means. You all hit your shot and then whichever is the best shot on each side is the ball you play. Or it was something like that.

I fluked my first shot and it started well left before coming up just short of the green. The Boss and I just looked at each other as if that was what we expected. The Sarge was rattled as he knew my shot was a fluke. He duffed his shot so he and the Boss played from the site of the Big Boss's shot. We were down in a birdie and the Big Boss had a par thanks to the sarge's putter.

I don't quite know how the handicap system works but we were six Stapleford points ahead by the tenth hole. At a little after 1.00 it started to rain. We got out our Police issue wet weather gear. The Boss got out his Pringle rainwear protector. Yes, now we did look very much like poor cousins. It stopped raining after a couple of holes so we could all put our wet weather gear away. The Big Boss still looked like a Posh relative with his Pringle Sweater on.

It did get better for the Big Boss as he pulled two shots back over the next few holes. He was the better player and his Eighteen handicap was the result of years of playing. As for the rest of us, we barely had a full year of playing this game between the lot if us! By the time we were on the Eighteenth we were seven Stapleford's ahead. We finished the Hole and the Boss suggested we all go up for a beer. The Big Boss reckoned he had a lodge meeting to go to, but he did shake our hands. He went off to this car and we all trooped upstairs to the bar. The Sarge ended up buying us all a beer and swearing he would never play with the Big Boss again. He wanted to enjoy his game. The Big Boss kept trying to tell him he was holding his right shoulder too high. Still we won and the Boss was happier than I had seen him in a while.

Monday

Monday was a beautiful day. A real Rotorua Winters day with bright Sunshine and just a touch of frost in the air. By midmorning all traces of the frost had gone, and it was a balmy 15 degrees. I looked forward to checking out the report by Tim about the Friday night rapist. There was nothing exciting to read about. The guy used a condom so there was never going to be DNA samples. Quite brutal in his attack on the girl and she had suffered a few bruises to her head and shoulders. He had been quite rough with his assault on her person and, how can I say this politely, he didn't bother too much about making sure she was ready for penetration. Fortunately the girl had participated in sexual activity before but I was still annoyed. I spoke to the Boss about the assault and he also reckoned we may have a second rapist on our books but it was probably a bit soon to tell.

Mike and I went around to see Ronnie and Shi Low. To be honest I was struggling to find things to do. Yes, we had the Murder case and the Armed robberies on our plate but until somebody left us a clue we could do nothing with them. I also had the new rape case on my plate but I was being a little held back by the Boss's reluctance to say it was definitely a different guy.

Ronnie was his usual cheery self when we arrived. We had rung prior so Ronnie had the kettle on. Mike was a little wary after his previous visit to Ronnie, but we sat and had a chat over a cuppa. Ronnie wasn't able to assist us in our enquiries, but he did say he'd had a meeting with 'Tohi' who was his opposite number at the Black Power gang. It seems that neither of them wanted an all-out gang war so they had met and decided that the current drug service levels would stay in place and neither of them would be approaching the other's clients to try and grab more trade. I jokingly asked Ronnie how long he reckoned that would last. His reply was to the effect that when the gangs fought there were often innocent passersby who got hurt. He would not be the one to break the truce, but he would have something to say if the Opposition got a bit greedy.

Ronnie then went on to say he had been made aware that the Black Power gang had been actively recruiting in Town. There was only one conclusion he could draw from that. At some time in the next six months The Black Power would try to take over Rotorua from the Mongrel Mob. It would mean a possible all out gang war if he could not nip it in the bud. He would keep me appraised of any developments, but we were to take that as our warning. That is just what I needed!

I filed this info away to mention to the Boss and then we had lunch.

After Lunch we went to meet with Shi Low. As usual Mike was kept outside the office while I was served tea inside Shi Low's office. Shi Low had nothing to really say to me. Business was satisfactory across all of his traders. He did have a concern about the Armed Robberies that were going on in Town, but he assured us that no Chinese Dairy owner had yet been taken advantage of. He hoped that would continue to remain the case. I really don't think he was threatening the Law, but I would hate to see what Shi Low would have done to our armed Robbers. I mentioned to Shi Low that we had not had a repeat of the coincidence where five people had all broken the pinky finger of their left hand for over a month. His reply chilled me a little. As he drank his cup of tea Shi Low said Our people are sad about hearing that your potential shoplifters perhaps have broken a finger. Let it be known that among our people we will not get into the habit again of breaking the same finger each time. Not that we would ever take your law into our own hands. I was somewhat at a loss for words to say. Shi Low had as good as indicated to me that he would not break the same finger each time. He had not said he would not break the finger of shoplifters. He had said he would break a different finger each time almost in order for the guys at the hospital to not recognize a pattern of events happening.

I knew I would not be able to persuade Shi Low to let the police deal with it, so I thanked him for his efforts and finished my tea. On the upside I was not dismissed quite the way I had been dismissed previously.

Walking back to the Office, Mike asked me what had gone on in Shi Low's office. I explained to him that while Shi Low was not directly challenging the Police force, he did have a reputation for sorting these things out by his own means. It wasn't a slur on the Police, more it was a way of keeping his reputation intact. They preferred to deal with their problems in their own way.

Once back at the Office I filled in the Boss and the Sarge on the updates I had been offered by Ronnie and Shi Low. The Sarge could remember when they last had a gang war in town. It was in '05 and the Sarge had still been on the beat. It was a bad time when a gang member could be gunned down in broad daylight in town and drive by shootings were common enough to not make the TV news.

Shi Low, the Sarge put down as posturing.' He has to keep his locals in order so he has to say there will be consequences or he won't keep getting his dollars for protection.'

That brought five O'clock up and I went home. No new armed robberies and no new murders. I remember thinking to myself it was only a matter of time.

Chapter 9

The Judge felt his inactivity had been vindicated. Yesterday's sermon by the new Minister had centered on the subject of the 'end of times'. This was from the Book of revelations and the Judge thought that the minister had captured the tone admirably. It was held that when the end of times was due there would be so many signs available to the true believers. There was already the sign of the beast, '666' everywhere in the barcodes. Women were flaunting their bodies in an attempt to tempt those men who were not true believers. It basically was just a matter of the four horsemen of the Apocalypse riding down the streets of Central Rotorua to make it a clean sweep that the 'end of times' were upon us.

As always, the Judge was pleased that the minister had specifically referred to those brazen women flaunting their bodies as just another sign of the times. He was the one doing something about that sign. If anything, he was aware that he was the only one trying to make that point. If only he could make more women understand the danger, they were in and what perils they would indeed face on the day of judgement. The Judge had already selected his next target who he would try to convince to change her ways. Her name was Susy. Yes, she dressed in a provocative manner but there was something else about her that bothered him. She seemed to enjoy the effect she was having on the men she walked among. She was definitely not a whore. Neither did she seem to be a jezebel. To use the local term she was a tease. He had already followed her home on two occasions, and she was so full of herself she had not noticed that he was following her. She would have to pay for her sins or at least convince the Judge that she was penitent.

Tuesday

It was another nice day in Rotorua. Sunny but without the touch of frost they had gone through the previous day. I was in at my usual time and the Boss was running late. He had gone to see one of his CI's to see if they had come up with anything concerning the two cases that were on our plate.

The Boss's CI had known about a general whisper in the air about the gang of armed robbers. He sort of knew the driver of the getaway car. Once Dollars had swapped hands the Boss had a new lead.

The new lead had a name and that was Rangi Totara. He was well known to us. He had a sheet that included Violence, car theft, domestic assault, burglary and arson. Although the Arson charge related to a car theft, he had then torched to destroy evidence.

We had a get together and discussed how we would handle this lad. We did not have any evidence relating to the armed Robberies and the fact he was a smoker didn't make it easier for the Boss to make any head way on arresting him. According to the Boss "Smoking is still not a bloody crime, even if it should be!"

We decided to put a tail on him for a couple of days and see if he aroused any suspicion. Mike and Derek were allocated to that job. Mike drew days and Derek drew the night shift.

It was at that point we got a call from the Big Boss. It seems they were having a meeting on the Ohinemutu Marae today to discuss how Police and Māori could work better together. Obviously there was a longwinded Māori name for it but it was expected that the Boss and the Big Boss would attend. And if I had nothing to do, I should probably attend.

Try as I might, if the Boss was going to be saddled with it, I was also going to be roped into it as well.

The Sarge was trying to hide his smirk once he knew what was going on.

We had to be there at 10.00 to be welcomed onto the Marae. I had already been welcomed on, but I was still classed as a visitor of some importance to the discussion, so I still had to be welcomed on along with the Boss. The Big Boss was classed as a local, so he was on the welcoming committee. If you have ever been welcomed onto the marae you will know it's a matter of face.

I had a lucky day. Other than the greetings and the like, not a lot was in Māori so I could understand it. Don't think badly of me. I was in a place where I really didn't belong to so I was prepared to do my bit but if the whole thing had been in Māori I would have been like a spare part.

It was a good time in that I enjoyed myself and the local elders did take some part of accepting the blame for their young offenders. I wanted to shout out 'get real' when they started on about the offenders going back to the old tribal ways of something and something. These kids lived in a modern world with modern values. Telling them to go and practice their Taiaha in preference to going on the internet was, to me, approaching the problem from the wrong angle. To me it was the Tribes that needed to get more modern and embrace what the world had to offer. But then again, what did I know about their problems. At one point I did end up face to face with the Chief Inspector. It was awkward! I wanted to remind him about our win on Sunday. He seemed happy to be talking about the problems that modern Māori youth face. I'd guess he was doing his thing as the local Police chief. As for me it was taking me away from my real job which was solving crimes! I probably also mended a few fences on the Marae. Last year I had helped put away one of their locals who was giving the kids a good hiding, or his mate was. I was spoken to warmly by the people I met. Maybe they thought the local guy was adding to their problem. Whatever happened I enjoyed my day, and I did not get abused by any of the locals.

I almost reckon the Boss might have enjoyed the day. We ended up with a few new initiatives to curb Māori Crime Rates and most of them were for the Marae to handle. At least it wasn't down to the local law to come up with a solution! That has to be a plus.

Wednesday

We had a quiet day. Mike and Derek had followed the new lead and had not come up with a great deal. The villain had visited one of the lads we thought might be involved in the Armed Robbery ring. He had been there for a half hour and then gone on his way. There was a debate about whether we should put the new lad under surveillance but we decided to stay with the lead that the Boss's CI had given him. The Boss added me to the list of lads watching this new lead. As I was a DS I had the day shift from 8.00 to 3.00. Mike had the evening shift 3.00 to 8.00 and Derek had the late shift from 8.00 until the guy went to bed. We figured it was not worth watching him when the dairies were closed.

I watched the new lead until 3.00. Again he had visited the home of the guy we had thought may be involved. At 7.00 he went to the pub. At 11.00 he was way too pissed to drive so he walked home.

Chapter 10

The Judge had followed the girl home from the pub and she was still walking with a twirl to her short skirt that would have any man thinking lustful thoughts. He followed her down to her driveway, it was a right of way, and he knew he would only have the one chance to surprise her as the Driveway offered no real cover.

He counted to 5 and then followed her down the right of way. There was something wrong! She should have been at her front door. He could now see the lights coming on from the back of the house. The slut had gone round and let herself in at the back door. He could see the girl as she wandered around the house pulling curtains and drawing the blinds. He followed her path to the back door and the stupid girl had left it unlocked. The Judge thought that was probably a consequence of being under the influence of Alcohol. It was just another thing she would have to repent about. As he thought about the girl, the lounge lights went off, the hallway and then her bedroom light went on. The Hallway light was turned off and the Judge knew she was getting prepared for bed.

He decided that tonight was the night she would repent so he waited for a full five minutes to allow her some decency before he entered the house. He crept down the hallway just as the girls bedroom light went off.

He had rehearsed this moment many times before in his imagination. If he leaped onto the bed, he would have her face duct taped so fast she would be stunned for a moment. That would give him a good opportunity to tape her arms to the bed or the bed head. Then he could begin to chastise her for her loose ways. Yes, he might also have to commit a sin of murder if she did not repent. But he knew he would give her every chance to make a genuine repentance. This girl was a harlot and needed to be reminded of her obligations.

He did manage to leap on top of her and surprise her with Duct tape across her mouth. While she struggled ineffectively, he also got both of her arms tied to the bedhead with the same duct tape. When she calmed down, he realised she was naked. This girl did not even wear pyjamas to bed! What more evidence did he need!

He struggled to speak to her as she was, well, naked. Her breasts were there in full view, and they were of a pleasant size. Certainly in keeping with the rest of her body. Immediately he thought of her body he went into another struggle internally. He was supposed to the Judge and yet here he was ogling at this woman. Roughly he pulled the bedclothes up to cover her nakedness. Was it to just be contrary as she immediately lifted her legs and pushed the bedclothes down so he could see her entire nakedness.

He could see her secret parts. She was moving suggestively. He ripped the tape off her mouth and was about to say 'repent, woman!" when she said to him. "You want a piece of this don't you."

He did want her so badly and he was more than ready to enter her when she said again. "If you want a piece of this, help yourself. Go on, go for it!"

He could not help himself. He entered her and yet he was still determined to cast his seed onto the belly of a whore. There is something of a rushing of blood to the head when a man ejaculates. He so desperately wanted to cast his seed onto her belly as the good book said. Instead he suffered a rush of blood, and he filled her with his seed. He did notice that during his fit of lust he had taken off one of his gloves. He knew in himself that it was to better let him feel the breasts of this harlot. Was there no end to this trial? He had felt the woman's breasts, both of them, and they had felt so good to him. Was there to be no end to this trial for him?

It can take anything up to twenty seconds for a man to come back from his mini death experience when he ejaculates. The Judge took at least twenty seconds. As his hearing returned he heard her saying something like, "well, that was quick!"

He knew he would have to kill her. As well as everything else she was a Whore because she had just let him use her. And she was a Jezebel! And a Harlot. He was still inside her as he reached forward and strangled her. It should be quick, he told himself. She should be killed but because he himself had somehow failed the test he had put himself under, she deserved it to be quickly over and done with. He accomplished his act of judgement quickly and with minimal fuss.

When he thought back to what had just happened, he was horrified. He had been tempted by the devil and he had failed the one test he should have passed. He sat up and his member was flaccid and a little sticky. He got up and left the bedroom in a daze. He grabbed a bottle of orange juice from the fridge and took a mouthful to clear away the taste he had in his mouth, He couldn't wash it away as it was the taste of failure. He had been tested and he had failed.

Thursday

Yes, I had a lazy day the day before, but I still objected to being woken at some time just after midnight. It was the Boss. "We've got another murder and it looks like our lad. The address is...... I'll see you there." With that the phone went dead. I cursed as much at a new murder as I cursed at being woken in the middle of a deep sleep. I was having a good dream that involved Tiff. She was being naughty and warranted some punishment. I was just getting to the punishment part when the phone rang! Why does the damn phone ring when you are getting to the good part!

When I got to the scene in Aquarius Drive, Mike and the Boss were already there along with two Squad cars and an ambulance. Mike had asked the Boss to be called when a murder was first reported. As far as I was concerned it was another good mark for Mike that he wanted to be so involved. As far as the Boss was concerned, if he had to be up and about in the middle of the night then I and Mike could also reap the benefits of being early on the scene. One of the squad cars was a K9 unit and the boss was keen for no one to spoil the scent for the dog. The K9 went immediately to the left of the driveway and followed the scent for perhaps 100 meters and then he doubled back. Reaching us again, the Dog Unit cast around for a new scent and quickly went to the right of the driveway. Again he might have led his handler for 100 meters and then returned to his starting spot.

The Handler was confused. "We have one of two things going on. Either he walked up and down the street and at some time he got into a car and drove off. Alternatively he may still be inside and hiding in a wardrobe or something."

That got the Boss in a pickle. He wanted to get into the house, but he knew we had to be careful. The Guy may still be inside, and he may be armed. The second Squad car let us know he had a firearm in his boot so the Boss decided we would go in behind the armed Squaddie and search the place. We found the girl in the main bedroom. She was dead but we still had to search the rest of the house first.

When we had established that the house was empty other than the victim, we could now go in and deal with the Victim. It was a necessary nuisance, but it probably took twenty minutes to make sure that the house was clear. It was twenty minutes we could have spent looking for the murderer.

Once we had established the girl was dead, we let the fingerprint lads have a first sweep of the house. Although the house was covered in the victim's prints, we did find a few extra fingerprints. There was a print on the bedside table we were unable to identify and a nearly complete handprint on a carton of orange juice in the fridge. The Print lads said they would be available on our database by midday. The Ambulance had a callout, so it was after two when they got back, and we released the Body for Mike at the Morgue to do his thing. The Boss and I were stood outside when I asked the question, "Who called it in?"

The Boss reckoned it was a mate of the victim's. Said she would ring late at night and always got a reply. It was unusual for the girl not to reply. When the Operator at 911 suggested she leave it until morning, the caller sounded very agitated, so she had sent out a squad car to double check and they had come up with no answer, yet the kitchen light was on. That was when we had been called. Although they were not aware a murder had been committed, there was something that the Boss had caught on the tone of the operator.

I asked the Boss why the K9 unit was there. It was something that Derek suggested at their discussion last week. He reckoned if we got a K9 unit on the scene we might be able to determine which way the Assailant headed and then perhaps we could get a number plate off the car. I said that might be clutching at straws, but the Boss reckoned it was a small price to pay for developing a good keen copper! As always, I agreed with the Boss.

Mike and I and the Boss agreed we should not get in before 9.00 that morning with such an early start. I don't know about the rest, but I slept like a log until my alarm went off at 8.00.

The Big Boss had called the Sarge just after 8.00 looking for answers to the questions he was being asked by the local papers. When the Sarge said the Boss would not be in until later, he left the message that the Boss had better call him ASAP. When the Boss arrived, he decided to ignore the Big Boss for a half hour. He also liked the morning ritual of having a decent cup of coffee in peace before tackling the rest of the day. We got a preliminary call from Mike at the Morgue. It seems the victim had been raped and then strangled. Hopefully he will have his Prelim report available for us by midafternoon. I was looking at my own version of the various reports and I was coming to the conclusion that this was probably the guy who had done the previous rapes but not the one who had raped the girl at the end of Luke Place. It definitely had a different MO about it.

When the Boss had finished his Coffee, he rang the big Boss. Under instructions to come and see him straightaway, the Boss disappeared upstairs. He didn't look that pleased about going!

When the Boss returned for upstairs he disappeared into his office. He was supposed to come up with a list of things he had been doing to catch the murderer. Between him and the big Boss they had to find something to tell the local papers.

The Sarge rang Jane, the Big Boss's PA, later in the day. She reported that the Boss and the big Boss had a fiery discussion. When the Big Boss said something about having to speak to the papers it appears my Boss said something to the effect of "Not my Problem."

That may not have been the answer the Boss was looking for, as it went rapidly downhill after that. The Boss and the Big Boss were arguing and among the topics covered were the fact that Dave Powell had passed his exam and should be congratulated. The Boss reckoned it was the first he had heard of Dave passing the exam. The Big Boss is reported to have then said, 'well I am telling you now!" The Boss said something back to the effect that he did not think Alan Kirk was cut out for CIB work and the office was over manned and Dave Powell should be transferred. I have to say that I agreed with the Boss. Dave had only three calls to deal with in his five weeks of shift work. Tim Cross had some busy nights and quiet nights, but he had notched up over forty calls in total. As always one thing led to another and now, we were forming a special task force to deal with the murders. As ever I am a humble servant who is there to cover the desires of my overlords. It would depend on how the Boss decided to respond to the Big Boss's call to set up a task force as to how much of an onerous task it would be. Given the Boss's response of 'You lot' I didn't figure we were going to work that hard on setting up this new task force. If there was any comeback, I am sure the Boss and the Big Boss would get it sorted out.

After an hour in his office the Boss came out and the minions in the office, including me, tried to look like we were busy doing important work. He collared Mike and I and suggested that we could consider going to this church service on Sunday. It would give us a chance to have a look at the place and possibly suss out anyone we recognised or was acting a bit dodgy. We did have some footage of the Belgian bar and their Country music night. If we recognised anyone from that footage it may give us a starting point to work from.

The Sarge overheard our chat and was on the phone to the Springfield Golf Club. Could we change our tee time from Sunday to Saturday? Not a problem. New tee time of Midday. All organised. It seems that Sarge was quite enjoying his morning at the Golf Course. I had noticed a few weeks previous that he was eying up a new set of clubs. He was getting keen, but I did know that Huia, his wife, would not go for a brand new set of clubs until he sold the boat that was blocking their driveway.

The Sarge also said he would consider going with the three of us to the church. Between the four of us we should be able to cover the whole congregation. I wasn't thrilled with the Boss's Suggestion that I give up my one day off to go to Church, but I had to go along with it.

In the midafternoon we got a call from Mike at the Morgue. He had his prelim report available if we wanted to go up and see him.

The Boss told Mike and I to follow him out to his car. He did give Mike a roasting about how he nearly puked the last time we were at the morgue. Mike promised not to puke so the Boss let him come with us.

Mike, from the morgue, was all business but was more concerned with finding out what we had discovered about the Murderer. The Boss reckoned we would tell Mike after he told us about the Autopsy.

"Death by Strangulation. You can see the hand marks around the throat here and here." He said this as he was pointing to the body of this very naked and lovely girl laid out before us. I thought it was a bit off but this was 'Mike from the Morgues' world and he only saw things as being alive and worth looking at and dead and also worth looking at. Mike continued, "Also, you may note the bruises on her arms. If I was a detective and I'm not, I'd say he pinned her down by her arms and then he taped her to the bedhead or something like that. I'd say this guy was fairly fit. He does seem to have got her in her bed but there's no sign of a real struggle. If it was left to me I'd say she was in bed when he arrived. Of course I won't say that in the report. I only say the facts but if you want my opinion?" He left the rest unsaid, then he moved on to the other parts of his report.

"She has been raped. Evidence of a possible forced entry but it may have been consensual. I can't really determine that. Can I just say that she may have consented but the assailant might have been a bit quick for her. Victim had been drinking but was not inebriated. Estimated time of death between 10.00 and midnight. What else do you need?"

Thankfully he did not ask us to scan her lower body parts for signs of entry. I reckon that might have finished Mike Jackson off. He was already a bit green around the gills!

"That covers what we need, Thanks Mike. I had a word with the Boss yesterday and you shouldn't be getting any more calls from him."

With that we left the Morgue and went back to the office. It was interesting that among the things covered in his chat with the Big Boss yesterday, he had also managed to include the fact that he did not want the Big Boss speaking to Mike's boss. It certainly seems to have covered a few topics that my Boss wanted to clear up. I suppose when you have a bust up, that is the best time to bring up all of the bits you need to say, rather than being polite about everything. In a way I could sort of understand the Boss and the Big Boss's relationship. Every so often they need a shouting match to clear the air and get out what had been bothering them for a few days.

It was now late in the afternoon, so we called it a day.

Friday

We really had no new leads to go on. The local paper, the Daily Post had a headline about there being a new victim in town. As well as the rape the girl had also been murdered so there was no end of juicy stuff for the paper to work on. I tossed up whether to go and see Ronnie but decided against it. I had nothing to discuss with him and I had already told the Boss about my last conversation with Ronnie about him and the Black power making an arrangement. The Boss anticipated there would be trouble in a month or two, but he had the Murders and the armed robberies on his plate at the moment. He would deal with Ronnie's problems next month. At that point the Boss's phone rang and it was the Minister at the Church we had visited last week. He had got back from his time away and had spent much of the last week ringing back his parishioners who first rang to say the Minister and his mother were in their prayers. When she had died the calls became sympathy calls and repeating that he was in their prayers.

The Boss and I went to see the Minister at his Manse in Hillcrest. He welcomed us very warmly and invited us in. He apologised for his tardiness in replying again and the Boss said it was completely understandable. Now this guy, whose name was Pete, was completely surprised by the Boss's opening statement.

"Pete, we believe that a member of your congregation may be a murderer. Got any thoughts?"

Pete was understandably blown away. He spoke in that way that did not need anyone else to help with the conversation. "Wow. A murderer you say. And he's in my congregation. Sure it's not a female?"

I was happy to let the Boss carry this chat. "Well last night we believed he raped a female and then strangled her. So I would prefer to think it was a male."

"Hmm. Raped and then strangled her. Was it local or at least here in town. Yes, sounds like a male but I can't think of anyone who would do something that horrible. And definitely not a part of my congregation."

The Boss added. "Is it perhaps something to do with your sermons. You know, hellfire and brimstone and damnation. Would that incite someone to er... do this...act?"

Pete laughed. "I'm flattered you think my sermons would have that affect but there are way better speakers than I and they do not have that effect on their flock."

The Boss than asked him if he would have any objection to a couple of squad members taking a look and listen in on Sunday's service.

Pete was quite happy. "Absolutely not a problem. I decided to go with hell fire and Damnation sermons as it was a fairly new church, and it does have Fundamental in its title. No, please do come along and have a look and a listen. I look forward to seeing you there."

The Boss did ask. "Can I ask what does the title of your church indicate? it's the Fundamental Church of God?"

"Basically we believe in the original bible and not the adulterated version. So it's back to the basics Women should be servants to the men, though I do not emphasise that side. No Homosexuals and that type of thing"

"No gays in your church, then?"

Pete laughed again. "No gays, no money lenders. Though I don't know how I would handle it if a gay guy turned up at the door. I would have to ask him to repent his sins and then I would have to believe him. That's an interesting point, maybe I'll do a sermon on gays in the mainstream churches. They seem prepared to take anybody who will fill the collection plate, nowadays."

The Boss's final words to Pete were along the lines of not doing the Gays sermon on Sunday. Pete agreed and said he would come up with something else.

We got back to the office around 11.00. I had suggested to Mike and Derek that they go around to the Secondhand dealers again. It was as much to get them out of the office and looking busy as it was anything else. I knew that once the Big Boss and my Boss had discussed the situation with Alan Kirk he would be gone. It was just a matter of time. Mike and Derek were out of the office.

What I did not expect was a memo from the Big Boss being passed to my desk telling us that Senior Constable Dave Powell was up for a transfer and Alan Kirk was to be switched back to the Squaddies patrol. Don't get me wrong. I did expect the memo from the Big Boss but certainly not as soon as it arrived. The Sarge was all set to have a few drinks for Dave Powell, so we organised to go out that night. Meet at 7.00 at the Belgian bar and we would take the evening wherever it took us.

I thought I would give Janet a ring and she was happy to hear from me. We arranged to meet later that day so I kept myself busy with paperwork until my time with Janet.

When I er... sat down with Janet, she told me she had that religious bloke back again last week. She was quite unabashed about what she did for her living, and it was something of a shock to be told so casually that the religious bloke had come back again. Evidently, he had stipulated that he wanted to ejaculate on her stomach rather than the usual thing. He said it was something the vicar had suggested. She went along with it and the guy was quite happy when he handed over his dollars. Janet once again thought the guy was a creep and wanted him to get on with it and finish as soon as possible. I asked her how she felt having sex with this guy and she reckoned it was all part of having sex with different blokes. Some are more enjoyable than the others but she was just one of those girls that loved having sex with different blokes. I wouldn't say she was a sex addict but she did fill in most of the criteria. Maybe she was a sex addict and she was using me as part of her addiction. To be honest, I didn't really mind about it.

Janet and I did our usual thing, and I was happy to be going home with a smiling face until I remembered Sarge's suggestion for the evening. Dave was a good guy, so I didn't mind helping him celebrate. I don't remember that much from the evening's entertainment so it must have been a good night.

Saturday

I turned up at Springfield in time for my usual practice on the putting green. Saturday at a Golf club is way busier than a Sunday. Maybe I was a little self-conscious or maybe I was still a bit tiddly from last night but I wasn't in the best shape. The fact that there were people watching me put me off my game! I'll blame that. I duffed my shot off the first tee and recovered for one over par. I might say that there were a half dozen blokes watching me tee off plus a foursome walking to the 11th tee. After that it seemed that on most of the tees there was a group behind us. It was probably the same group, but it affected my game. I shot a 108. The Boss hit a 99 and the sarge hit a 97. The sarge's 97 still did not beat my previous weeks score of 95 but I had a shocker and ended up paying for the Beers. My two partners were both happy with their scores, but I told myself to not play on a Saturday again.

Sunday

On Sunday I went to church, which is not something I would have expected to ever write down. The four of us decided to sit apart and keep an eye on most of the congregation. I was sat at the back, and I had a good view of most of the people in front of me.

It was a friendly church. Most of the people were from the Islands. Cook Island or Samoa or something like that although there was a fair few white looking people in the mix. The Sermon was fascinating. He started off with the Dan Brown book. The one called the DaVinci code. I had read it at some time, and it was a good read. Still a work of fiction but enjoyable. He started off with the suggestion that Mary was a fairly wealthy lady who had befriended Jesus. He went on for a minute then he tossed the Book off the pulpit. It made a loud noise as it hit the floor a couple of meters down. Then the minister turned to the Bible and read that part of the apostles out which mentioned Mary Magdalene. Then he told us to believe the Bible and that Mary was a whore. I think his intention was to infer that if Whores were loved by Jesus who were we to cast them down as lower people. I drifted away as my attention was attracted to several of the possible suspects in the congregation. I noticed that a few of the guys were being held by the Ministers oratory. I mentally tagged them as suspects or not suspects. I found myself looking at the congregation and dismissing guys as 'Too old' or "Too fat to jump on a bed without the bed collapsing'. You get the picture. When the plate came round, I gave $5.00 as I had enjoyed the sermon. The lady next to me thought I was being a bit mean as she put in her offering envelope.

On the way out the minister was stood at the exit greeting people as they left. He shook my hand and called me Mark as I left, then he moved on to the next person.

Outside the Church the Boss, the Sarge and Mike and I gathered around the corner to discuss what we had thought of the congregation. None of us had found it overly satisfying as a police exercise as we found ourselves listening to the Ministers sermon. I was glad I was not the only one!

Chapter 11

The Judge thought long and hard about the Ministers sermon on Sunday. Yes, the Minister had marked Mary Magdalene as a whore. But there was something else in his message. Was it respect for even someone as low as a whore? Was he talking to him and chastising him for killing that tart from last week? Was he saying it was fine that he go with a whore provided he spilled his seed on the outside. He knew he should not bring it up with the minister, but he was in something of a quandary. He decided after a lot of thought that he would perhaps visit a Whore again this week. Maybe it was appropriate for him to visit with a whore, and he would then be able to listen closely to the Ministers message next Sunday. Now should he go and visit with the same whore or should he try someone different. He fancied visiting somebody different and then he spent a few moments deciding what she would look like before realising he had fallen in the trap again. He was again having lustful thoughts. It was so easy to fall into this trap, he thought. He would just ring the first name in the adult entertainment ads. He was only there for one thing anyway. To give him a release so he could more clearly focus on his mission.

Monday

It was a murky day, and it didn't look like it was going to get better. The Sarge brought us our coffee and we sat and discussed the Sunday service with Mike. Derek was walking past and mentioned that it was a long time since we had all been to Church on a Sunday. What was happening? The Boss filled him in on the latest development. When I suggested we should go and see the Minister again Derek suggested I would be better off leaving it until tomorrow. The last time they had tried ringing the Churches on a Monday they had no success. Tuesday was a better day as the ministers took Monday off, usually. The Sarge reckoned he had read somewhere that the ministers had their weekly round of golf on a Monday. The Boss reckoned that was because the ministers wanted peace and quiet on their day off. Also he referred to some of my language as I consistently hit bad shots. He reckoned it might set a bad example if some of their parishioners heard their minister use some of the language I had used on the Saturday. I think he was joking. I hope he was joking!

We got the tox screen back on Monday along with the DNA/mRNA coding. As yet they were unmatched with any Criminal on our database. That was a positive. At least we knew the Murderer was not on our database. That just left us with around 4,500,000 other suspects to trawl through.

Alan Kirk was on his last week with us and had elected to rejoin the weekday shift. Dave Powell was still suffering just a touch from the excesses of Friday night and was now back on the Day Shift. There was a rumour that Dave had been headhunted by the Invercargill office if he didn't mind going down to the Deep south. The Boss had left things with the Big Boss to iron out and no one knew who would pull the Saturday and Sunday day Shift.

I don't think we did much for that day. Dave said he would cover the Saturday and Sunday Day shift as it would only be for a few weeks until his move. He was seriously thinking about moving to Invercargill. Having come from Sunny Auckland we did our best to dissuade him, but it was inside his head, so we left it.

That night I got a call from the Desk sergeant at the Squad room desk. It seems our rapist had been busy again. I got the address which was on the football field at kea Street. It's a short cul de sac at the lower end of Mallard drive. There was already a squad car there and I said I would be there in ten minutes.

As far as I could tell the girl had been walking along Mallard Drive and had been forcibly pushed to the soccer field on Kea Street. Where he had tried to get up to his usual stuff. She was lucky. While he was forcing her to the ground a local had been walking his dog on the soccer field and the assailant had been disturbed. This was at something close to midnight so the offender had gotten away while the Local helped the girl up to her feet. Let's just say she had been sexually assaulted during her brief time on the field. The ambulance was patching her up from her grazes so it was a few minutes before I got to speak to her. I spoke to the local guy who had been the hero of the moment and got his story before speaking to the girl. She wanted it all hushed up, understandably, as she didn't not want to be named, and in her words, and shamed. I told her she would have to make a statement but she would have to convince the local not to ring the papers. Fortunately he was happy to keep things quiet. So I had a statistic for another sexual assault and I could count myself lucky it had not been worse!

Tuesday

On the Tuesday I reported into the Boss and the sarge. On the upside it was close to where the previous sexual assault had been so could it be linked? On the downside I only had a gut feeling this was the second guy and the not religious fanatic we had been chasing.

What time do ministers get out of bed? That was the question we asked ourselves as wondered when to ring the Minister. The Boss decided we would leave it until 9.00 which we did and were invited round for a morning coffee at 10.00.

Again we were warmly welcomed, and we sat round his dining table while we drank our coffee. The issue of helping the Police with their enquiries came up and Pete had a problem.

As Pete had explained "most of our congregation are lower socio economic. Many of them are Islanders with perhaps 40% or maybe even 50% are white. Would it surprise you to know we have a few Overstayers in the Flock? Perhaps the only time we will see our MP is when he comes around grubbing for Votes at election time. And you are asking what? Get everyone in our congregation to have a DNA test? Perhaps you would prefer them to just give their Fingerprints. Before you get round to asking the question, let me ask you first. Why should they put themselves in the Government noose when there is nothing in it for them."

I let the Boss answer that. Well, that's what he gets the big dollars for!

"Yeah, you are right, Pete. I suppose I could make a big appeal to you to be civic minded?"

Pete laughed and shook his head.

"What about if I said it would be a great way to show your congregation what a leader you are, if you went first?"

Even the Boss couldn't help but laugh at this one. "No, you are totally right, Pete. It's on us to come up with something that appeals and as yet, we are drawing a zero. Leave it with me and I'll get onto it, but we do feel you may have a murderer in your midst." Thanking Pete for the coffee we left and drove back to the Station. Pete was still skeptical about the murderer being in his congregation.

That afternoon we had a meeting with everyone who was available.

The Boss started with. "Right! We reckon our main murder suspect is a member of this fundamentalist church up on Sunset. The DS also has a guy getting his jollies on random birds walking alone at night. Let's concentrate on the religious guy first. He's going the whole way and topping them if they don't promise to behave themselves. We get on Ok with the Minister. But his problem is that he may have a few overstayers in his flock. Also he may have recently done a sermon on the mark of the Beast, whatever the hell that is, and his members won't have a bar of anything that smacks of a barcode because he said it wasn't right for them. Have I got that right DS?"

"That sounds about right Boss. Also he has a thing about.... er... "When I realised what I was about to say I rather faltered.

"What the DS was about to say is that he also did a sermon on onanism. Look it up if you don't already know about it. I had to. Right?

How do we get this minister to co-operate with us. We need to look at his church records and he won't show them to us. Sarge, you can write on the board, and I can see we have a few suggestions already."

In terms of suggestions, the Sarge stood up to write on the Board and he was met with nothing.

"Come on Lads, the DS suggested. We have to get this bloke to talk to us. What about a religious nutter. Put that on the Board."

The Sarge responded. "I reckon if you stop calling him a religious nutter you might get a few brownie points.

The Sarge wrote on the Board 'Zealot'. When asked what it meant the sarge simply said it means someone who has Zeal. If they have Zeal they can be described as a Zealot. It sounds way more acceptable to a Christian follower than being called a religious nutter! I did have a look later in the day on Google. It seems that the 'Zealots' were a member of a fanatical sect during the first century AD. Their big thing was to stop the Roman Domination of what we now call Palestine. They promoted unrest against the Romans being the rulers of Palestine. I reckon the Sarge has it right with the modern day Zealots.

The Boss added. "Fit. When I looked at some of those lads in that church, I reckoned he would have to be fit otherwise the bed would collapse."

I added "So Fit and slim?"

"Exactly right," said the Boss.

"'How does he get or pick out these birds he kills. Does he have a delivery round? You know. Does he deliver around town and pick them out or does he deliver to businesses and picks them out at their place of work?"

"Good Point, Derek. DS have a quick look at the files. Do these birds work at a job or are they stuck at home?"

"Age." Said the Sarge.

"Upper age of this murderer. I'm going to say 50. Lower age maybe 20 or 25?" said Mike.

"I agree. 20 should be the younger end."

"Māori? Pasifika. Pakeha?"

"We think Pakeha because of his lack of an accent. Everyone we have spoken to reckons he was a Whitey. Although we have only spoken to one survivor. So let's leave that open ended."

I checked the Files. All of the girls had a job so we reckoned he may have a job where he delivers to commercial premises. I added 'Courier driver or Postie in Town'.

When I did a full check, I realised that Nichola had a job in the Suburbs so we amended the Courier driver to big letters.

By the time we had done a half hour on the board we were really getting somewhere. The Boss thanked us for our input. We decided to go and visit the Minister again in the morning. I called him and we agreed a time for the following day at Coffee time.

We had not heard of any new armed robberies for a week. I mentioned it to the Boss and he reckoned they were having a few days off. They will be back on our doorstep sometime soon.

Wednesday

We went up to Pete, the Ministers, manse on Hillcrest. He apologised for his frankness yesterday, but he did say he could only give us information with a clear conscience on his part. That was fine with us, so we sat down for our coffee. He had a list of his congregation members in front of him which we were not allowed to see. We fully accepted his reticence as he was effectively snitching on his congregation.

Pete again asked us for our criteria, and we said Male aged 20 to 50' His response was '61' and it took him a few minutes to get that amount.

Slim and probably reasonably fit. His response was down to '17'. I could see him mentally picturing these congregation members.

Māori or Pasifika or Pakeha. His response again was '17.'

Zealot. His response dropped to '8'. Now we were getting somewhere.

Has a job, maybe a courier driver. Maybe a Postie or a delivery driver. His response came down to '6'.

The Boss then asked for those six names. Pete reckoned he could only give us 3 of those names because the others were either overstayers or they might be paid under the table. The Boss chose to go with just those names at this point. If we could eliminate these names we would come back and try harder, but it was a start.

The three names were Colin Jessup, Johnny Scarrow and David Jones.

We got back to the station, and we gave the three names to each of the DC's and asked them to give us what they could on their name.

Derek was back first with his name, Johny Scarrow. Derek was always on the button when it came to searching for information. He seemed to know how to phrase his questions so that the computer would know what he was asking for. As far as I was concerned it was akin to black magic what he could get out of a computer.

Mike was the next and Alan Kirk came in last.

Johnny Scarrow was an interesting guy. A courier driver for an independent. Joined the church three years ago. Single. His income we estimated would be around $70,000 so he could afford to chuck a few dollars in the collection plate. His delivery route took him around town and out to the suburbs. He did domestic deliveries as well as commercial.

I looked at Colin Jessup next. Mike had covered this guy and he dug a fair bit of info on the guy. It seems he also worked for a courier but as an employee. It also seemed that Colin had a record with us. Well the Minister had not let on that information. Perhaps he did not know about Colin's record. Assault, GBH and a burglary but he turned religious a few years ago and had been clean ever since. I looked up

Colin's prints on the database and he was no match for the murderer. So we could wipe Colin off our list.

When I looked at David Jones, I was reminded of how poor Alan had been in our CIB room. He barely filled a half page in where the other two had gone into double pages. I quietly asked Derek to have a go at digging out more info on David Jones. Within a half hour he was back with a couple of pages of info. This was more like it. Dave was a Postie delivering around the town centre. Occasionally he would do a delivery day out in the suburbs, but it was a rarity. David had no record I could find. He had joined the Church around four years ago, he was single. If I had to pick one person out of the three, we were given, for whatever reason I would have picked David. Let's call it a hunch. I left the files on the Boss's desk and went home as it was after 5.00.

Thursday

For whatever reason, every time the internal phone rang, I thought it was a report of another armed robbery. We were overdue for another Dairy to be hit and it was bugging me. It was like waiting for your birthday and seeing your presents but not being allowed to open them until someone said so!

The Boss had discovered the files on his desk, and he walked out to me with a letter. "It seems only fair to give some paperwork back. You might be interested in that".

It was another piece of paper with the word 'Harlot' written on it. I had almost forgotten about the murder case last week because I was so wrapped up in the murder case! If that sounds a bit weird, it is. Let's say I am a bloke who can only concentrate on one thing at a time!

I looked at the Boss. It confirmed what we hoped and that was that we did not have another killer on the loose. Last week's murder was committed by the same guy. So why did he change his MO? I was thinking about why had he raped this last girl?

The Boss went back to his office and scanned the files thoroughly. He came out and asked me which one did I think our killer was.

I went for David Jones and the Boss was convinced it was Johnny Scarrow.

At least we now had a couple of names to follow up. The Boss called a meeting of the troops to determine what our next move would be. The consensus was that we put a tail on both of the guys. If they were working on a courier route, they would have to be in bed early. We would only need a couple of guys for each tailing. That gave the Boss a problem. He would still need to cover the weekend shift. I could see his mind working on the problem. He was mentally going upstairs to ask the Boss if we could hang on to Alan Kirk for a couple more days. I reckon he knew that the Boss would give him beans about his manning levels for the CIB room.

We decided that putting a tail on these two guys was probably the best move available to us so the Boss got Alan Kirk into his office. When Alan walked out and went home, I figured the worst, but it was fine. Alan had agreed to cover the weekend shifts and so went home for a day and a half of rest. Alan was an odd lad. He may eventually decide to move up the ranks but as for now he was happy to do anything he was told.

Next the Boss went upstairs to see the Big Boss. I wouldn't have fancied being involved in that conversation. As it happened the Big Boss rolled over and gave my Boss permission once he had explained why he was doing it. Then the Big Boss started dropping hints about how he would like to have another game of Golf with us. This time it would be the Inspectors against the lower ranks. The Boss readily agreed as he had expected a fight over the new idea, he had for tailing these two new names. It was loosely agreed that we would set it up for the Sunday of the following week as the Boss wanted to get things organised with the tail over this weekend.

Derek and Mike would take the tailing of Johnny Scarrow. Dave Powell and I would take on the role of tailing David Jones. We tossed a coin and Mike and I got the day shifts. We had already worked out that our murderer worked mainly on a Wednesday evening so we decided that the tail should start on the Friday. And if you are wondering who would cover our normal CIB work, it was the Boss. He would have to cover everything that cropped up during the week. Just a little bit of me was happy that the Boss would be getting out and getting his hands dirty with a few assaults or Domestics etc.

Friday.

I was in at 7.00 on Friday and out at the courier depot by 7.15. With it being dark I was fine. It was when it got to a little later in the morning that I was having some difficulty. As David Jones job was being a Postie in the centre of town I stuck out like a sore thumb. I was quite reasonable at tailing someone but in this position, I was stuck between keeping an eye on the lad and not getting too close that he would spot me and my cover would be blown. Mike Jackson was having the same problem. Only with him, the Courier driver could park in unusual spots and be forgiven as he would only be there for a few seconds. Mike had a nice newish motor, so he was already behind the eight ball when he parked oddly and there were a few other people in town who let Mike know he was being inconsiderate. At 11.00 we called off the tailing as we were too conspicuous to be effective. We decided it would be better to tail them during the evening when they were at their most social or perhaps looking for the next victim.

Derek and Dave had the evening shift so we let them sleep and told them when they got in., They decided between them they would cover the evening detail until Wednesday and then we would swap. Mike and I decided we should go to the Church on Sunday morning and see if we could pick up any clues from the Ministers sermon and we could also keep an eye on the two lads while they were in their own 'comfort Zone.'

I mentioned to the Sarge that I probably would not be available for the Sunday game. He was on the Phone and had teed up a Saturday game for us within a few minutes. Tee time was a little earlier at 11.45

but I was still looking forward to it. Surely, I could not have two weeks in a row playing that badly?

With a bit of paperwork I managed to bring up 5.00. The Boss seemed to be out for most of the day chasing small crimes. It may do him good to hark back to the old days when he was a DC.

Saturday

Again I need to switch off when I know that people are watching me. I Shot a 106. The Boss got a 98 and the Sarge ended up top scoring with another 97. Yes I happily bought the beers but I had to do something about people watching me. In the Bar afterwards the Boss explained about FOWOPTOM and how it was affecting my game. Obviously, I asked what FOWOPTOM meant and he explained. "It's a human trait that most people suffer from it's called 'Fear of what other people think of me'. It's very common. You are so worried about what people think of your lack of experience in the game you subconsciously go to pieces. If you ignore them, like I do, you will soon realise that they don't give a stuff about your game. They are too busy worrying about their own game to worry about you. You do it on the Job as well. As soon as the Boss (the Big Boss) comes downstairs you try and look busy so you don't have to speak to him. Do me a favour the next time he walks into our office. Stand up and say 'Good morning, Boss' Then go and walk past him and go for a cuppa. He doesn't have a clue whether you walked in five minutes ago or five hours ago. He really doesn't care about you because he's too worried about himself. Oh and by the Way the Boss wants a return match next week."

Before the Sarge could start moaning, the Boss said "And don't worry about being on his team again. This time it's the Inspectors against the lower ranks. He reckons he might stand a better chance with me." There was the usual banter about who would win and I went home with something to think about. FOWOPTOM. Maybe I would give it a go.

Sunday

Mike and I met by arrangement, and we went into the Church. David Jones was sat very near the front of the pews and Colin Scarrow was sat about halfway back on the other side. I tucked myself in a couple of rows behind when I was asked to move my seat because this Samoan family always sat in that particular Pew. I wasn't in a mood for arguing so I moved and still had a good seat for watching David.

The Sermon was all about how we would know the end times were near. If I was to believe everything the minister was saying I would be cancelling my subscription to magazines and the like. Yes, it was for the masses gathered, but the longer it went, on the colder it left me feeling. I definitely did not belong here in this assembly. My mind wandered as I asked myself why I didn't belong here but I didn't come up with any great insights. David was following the words of the Minister avidly and I could not quite tell if he was filled with angelic fervor, or it was something he would think about over a beer. As I said, I was still having difficulty reading David. I still had him down as a good suspect though.

Monday

The Big Boss walked into our office, and I could see out of the corner of my eye that both the Sarge and the Boss were going to see how I would react. It was one of those moments. I got up and nodded to the Big Boss and went upstairs and had a cuppa. The Boss never even noticed my absence. He went into the Boss's office and bailed him up about our progress with the Murder and the tailing we were doing. As for me, I enjoyed my cuppa in the staff canteen. I used the time to think about what the Boss had said about 'FOWOPTOM'. I guess I was always aware of what other people thought about me but it seems I had overestimated my importance in the scheme of things. People were far too insecure about their own lives to worry about me. I resolved to try this thing out a bit more.

The Boss asked him for Alan for another week and he readily agreed. When My Boss told him what had gone on with the tailing the

Big Boss reckoned, we had made good decision and keeping a tail on both guys was a smart move on the Boss's part.

I don't know what was happening, but the Big Boss then went into the Squaddies office and gave them a cheery good morning. Asked a few questions and then disappeared up the stairs. He went in an office on that floor and wound his way back up to his office. He was on a meet and greet session and he wanted to make sure everyone was happy with his leadership. I'm guessing the last part, but it was strange for the Big Boss to leave his Ivory tower and mix with the lower lifeforms. As far as I was concerned I had faced a personal challenge and I had won.

When I got back to the CIB Room the Boss asked me if I wanted have a chat. I actually did feel a need to talk but I had nothing to actually say. There was so much going on in my head and I'm not just talking about the caseload we had on. The Boss said whenever you want to chat, just come in and close the door. That's what I liked about the Boss. It wasn't all about doing Police work and if I needed to chat about something, the Boss was always there for me.

Then the Boss told me that Shi Low had rung in my absence. Asking if I would return his call.

I rang Shi Low and got him at the first try. "Detective Sargeant. Thank you for returning my call. Could I invite you around to my office. Perhaps 2.00 on Wednesday would be convenient for you? Perhaps we could share some tea and discuss things of importance to us both."

I agreed to go and he asked that only I attend for a cup of tea. So Mike wasn't invited. What on earth could he want with me? I spoke about it to the Sarge, and he could only suggest that I should be punctual. When I spoke about it to the Boss, he suggested that ShiLow may have something to discuss about our murder or our Armed Robberies. Shi Low's people would be getting worried about the growing trend. Although no Chinese had been targeted there was always a possibility so obviously his people were a bit worried. Just don't be late. Shi Low takes it personally if you are late to a meeting with him.

Now I had the Boss AND the Sarge telling me not to be late I tried to push it to the back of my mind. My pushing was without success.

The Boss walked out of his office and made a suggestion. 'We have a print from this lad doing the murders. He's a courier. Why don't you get a parcel from him. It should have his prints on it and then we can eliminate him from enquiries?"

That actually was not a silly idea! so I then had to find out which companies used that independent Courier run. I found that out by ringing the local NZ Post so I ordered a parcel that would be perhaps a good size to go in my postbox and waited for it to arrive.

Derek and David were covering the night shift duty for tailing our two possible suspects. We had left the two suspects after the Church meeting with a puzzled look on their face. They were both wondering what the sermon meant to them. They may have been reflecting on the sermon's deeper meaning. To me they were both acting like suspects and wondering how it reflected on their 'mission.' I'm afraid when you have been around crims as much as I have you automatically tar them with the same brush as all criminals.

We had dropped the tailing of the suspects as being impractical and just kept up with the tailing of them after they finished work for the day. For our purposes it made it a lot easier to follow them under the extra cover of darkness.

<u>Tuesday</u>

I had a call from Dave Powell. He was tailing David Jones. Last night he had followed a girl home from work. He followed her on the Bus out to Moncur Drive. When she got off the Bus he followed her up Moncur drive where the girl lived. She was a financial planner for a local firm. Fit looking, as in very attractive. And living alone in one of those units on the right hand side. I thought she must be on a good income to be able to afford to live alone in Moncur drive. When

I checked the ownership records she was renting the place. Still she would need to be on a decent wage to afford a rental in Moncur Drive.

Derek had also rung the Boss. His lad Johnny Scarrow had also followed a girl home from work. She was a girl from what appeared to be computer entry or something like that. She was from a firm in View Road. She lived in Springfield Road a couple of doors down from the Shops When the Boss came out to tell me I was able to also pass on my info from Dave about David Jones. The Boss had remembered our chat from last week when we compared our suspects and said who we fancied as a villain. We still had our favorite villain and only time would tell us who was right. That is, if either of us was right.

I was struggling with a question on the senior Sarge exam so I spent a half hour with the Sarge while he tried to explain it. When that failed, I ended up with the Boss and he managed to get it into my skull. After that I was fine and managed to answer the paper quite easily. The Course paper consisted of a dozen papers of study and then each one had an at home paper to complete that asked questions relating to that particular paper. At the end of the Course I would have to then complete an exam under exam conditions but I was still a couple of papers away from that stage, yet.

Wednesday

It was a brilliantly fine day which usually meant we would have frost tonight.

Today I reminded myself that I had a meeting with Shi Low at 2.00. In at my usual time and served with a coffee by the sarge we all settled down and had our coffee while we discussed the events of the Day. The Boss said he had already had a call from Derek say that his lad had followed the same girl home as the previous evening. He had taken care not to be seen although the girl walked as if she only had herself to care about, so she would not have known if she was being followed.

He did ask if I had heard from Mike yet and when I said I had not, there was just a slight uplift of his head as if to say, 'I told you so'.

I almost hoped the Boss was correct. David did not seem like a bad lad, and he might have had a good reason for following the girl home. Now I am getting forgiving on the crims of our town. I have to stop thinking of them as innocent until proved guilty. With me it was easier to think of them as guilty until proved innocent.

The Boss finished his coffee and went into his office with the parting shot that I had better remember I had a meeting with Shi Low today. He shut his door and got on the phone.

For me I had nothing to do, really. I had a call from Mike Jackson. His tail had also followed the same girl home to Moncur drive. Only this time the suspect had hung around for a couple of hours. It almost seemed like he was making sure the girl did not go out again. It must have been around 9.00 pm that the guy turned around and walked back to the main road before calling a cab.

I was mentally preparing myself for the visit to Shi Low. It was unusual for him to ring me and make an appointment. At a couple of minutes to two I was walking up the stairs to see Shi Low and the doorman already had the door open for me. I was ushered straight into his office and within a few moments I was sat down opposite him while he poured the Tea. As always he remembered that I preferred milk in my tea. I've often thought that the great guys manage to remember all of the little details, such as if I preferred milk in my tea. For myself I have a memory like a sieve!

When I was comfortable he started to talk.

"Thank You Detective Sergeant for granting me your time today. I would assume you are wondering why I called you."

I responded as formally as I could think of. "It is always an honour for me to drink tea with Shi Low. And yes, I did wonder at your reason for calling me."

"Let me start by saying. I am wondering what word you would use. I want to say hypo-ethically for something you perhaps might imagine."

"Hypo ethically would be a word you could use but for the Police we might consider using the word Hypothetically."

"Thank you, Detective Sergeant. I shall use the word hypo-thetically. It is perhaps important we use your English words correctly. I would like you to imagine, hypo-thetically, that one of our people has worked hard and opened a shop on, shall we say, Pohutukawa Drive."

I was about to say there were no shops on Pohutukawa Drive but I remembered we were only speaking hypothetically. I asked him to continue. He smiled as If it appeared I was ready to play his game.

"This young couple have worked so hard and built up a reputation for scrupulous honesty as befits any member of my people."

Again I nodded in agreement. The Chinese were very hard working people. Perhaps they could sometimes be a little greedy with their margins, but they were a hardworking people.

"Let us suppose that we heard this shop, and these poor and hardworking people were about to become the latest victims of a holdup, such as we have read about in your local newspaper.

Again I nodded, all the while wondering where this was going.

"Let us say, hypo-thetically, that these people had heard of the crime about to be committed upon them. Would you imagine that these people would not prepare themselves for the robbery. Perhaps they may have a friend or two who would help them resist the robbery. Again we are only speaking hypo-thetically."

"I would imagine that could be a wise thing to prepare against." Where was this going?

"Detective Sergeant, I see you are letting your tea go cold. Is it not to your liking?"

I drank my tea and put the cup down on the fine table between us.

"More tea, Detective Sergeant?"

"I am full of your hospitality. Please do carry on."

"Where was I? Oh Yes. If these robbers did come into this Shop on Pohutukawa Drive. This Hypo-thetical shop. Would the Police do something?"

"Certainly they would. First, they would send a squad car to the scene and then we would have our Fingerprint squad around and they would take note of any Fingerprints and put it on our database."

"Let me ask you Detective Sergeant. You have had at least nine of these robberies on shopkeepers already. May I ask how many of these Robbers you have caught?"

"Well, we have a couple of them in custody awaiting trial. But after that we have to wait until they leave us a clue or something that we can work with."

"Thank you for your honesty, Detective Sergeant. So you have had nine robberies and you only have two people in your cells. That would seem a small reward for you after these gangs are causing so much consternation in the lives of these shopkeepers."

"We are bound by the laws of this land, Shi Low. You are aware as I am that we have to really catch them in the act of a robbery, or they may leave us a clue as to their identity."

"Thank you, Detective Sergeant. Fortunately, we are not so strictly bound by your laws. If we see someone robbing our store, we feel free to apprehend them and possibly deal with them."

"By 'deal with them' I would assume you mean chastise them. Possibly severely."

"Yes, it would be something like that."

"Are you telling me you would physically harm them?"

"Hypo-thetically Speaking. It is a possibility."

Shi Low topped up his teacup. He gestured to me to ask if I wanted more tea. I said yes. It seemed like a polite thing to say.

I started the conversation again. "So you would physically chastise these two people who entered your shop."

"There were three. If you remember the getaway driver. And of course this is all hypo-thetical."

My mind was racing as I tried to keep ahead of Shi Low. Yes, I knew I was coming second best but I had to try to keep on top of the conversation.

I continued. "So what if these people complained about your 'chastisement'? I mean to us, the Police."

"That is very unlikely!"

"Forgive me Shi Low. But I have heard of your chastisement of shoplifters. This sounds like you did more than break their fingers."

Shi Low looked at me straight in the eye. "It is perhaps safe to say these robbers will not rob another store. If you wanted to enquire further, their choice would not be of their own choosing."

Shi Low had just told me in no uncertain terms that he had either killed or maimed these guys who had robbed one of his shops. My initial thoughts were concerning how many Chinese Dairy owners I could think of. I quickly counted four and there would probably be more.

Shi Low leaned back in his chair. He knew the message had been received. It was up to me to finish our chat off so I would not lose face. I thought about this for a few moments.

"If these hypothetical people were ever found, would they have a story to tell us?"

Shi Low dismissed the idea with a wave of his hand. "They will never be found."

I was at a loss. On the one hand he had sorted out our spate of armed robberies. On the other hand he had topped three local lads, I assume, without a second thought.

I thanked Shi Low for his tea and frankness. He shook my hand, which was unusual, and then said for the final time "As always we are only Hypo-thetically speaking. Thank you Detective Sergeant for your time. I hope it was worth your while."

I thanked Shi Low and I was shown out of his office.

I left and took a slow walk back to the station. When I got back to the CIB office the Boss and the Sarge were waiting for me. I asked to go into the Boss's office and when the sarge hesitated I told him to come in as well.

As best as I could I relayed the conversation I had with Shi Low. The Boss's immediate comment was to the effect "Crikey, you could never say they were soft on crime!"

The Sarge just shook his head.

The Boss then said, "Well at least now you know why we haven't had any more armed robberies. Oh Hell. Now I have to mention this to the Boss."

It was only when the Sarge reminded that I realised I was duty that evening. One thing I did not want to do was tail someone for the evening. My head was in something of a muddle about Shi Low's treatment of the armed robbers. Fortunately the Boss saw my face and volunteered to do the evening duty if I promised to cover the CIB office in the morning. I was very grateful. Then the Boss did another decent thing. He told me to take the rest of the day off. He would also take the rest of the day off and pick up tailing David jones at 5.00. That left the Sarge in charge of the office. He did moan about it but the three of us had take some time to digest what we had just found from Shi Low.

I went home and tried to watch the Telly but that didn't work so I had an hour or so on my studies. I have to say that I was enjoying the mental challenge of my studies. It somehow focused my mind on something other than the constant thinking about the Rotorua Crims.

Mike had been in contact with Derek and got a pattern for what Johnny Scarrow did after work. The Boss rang Dave Powell. He had been contacted by the Invercargill office and it looked like he was heading South. Now there would be a mountain of paperwork to be dealt with and the like. The Boss also got an update on David Jones so he would know what to look for that evening.

Johnny Scarrow had followed his girl home after work to her place on Springfield Road. After a half hour he had gone home when it looked like his girl was settling in for the night.

David Jones was watching outside his girls place on Moncur Drive. He was careful in that he would walk up the road if anyone was walking up the street, but he would then return to his watching spot at the end of the girls right of way driveway. If anything was to happen, it would be tonight or tomorrow night, we guessed as that was when the Murderer had operated before.

The Boss was experienced in tailing a subject. He had four years' of work in Auckland, and they were often called in as being on the tail of someone. He was up in the circle at the top of Moncur drive and watching David jones through a garden shrub. That is, he was parked and sat in his driver's seat and watching David Jones though the edge of a Magnolia Shrub. The Boss had long learned how to turn the tailing situation to his advantage. He had to keep very still when the tail was walking up the road, but it was quickly back to his position when he needed to be.

For me I was having a quiet night. I had done an hour of study and that was enough to shut my brain down from remembering the conversation with Shi Low. I had settled down to watching the TV and I was in one of those moods where I was watching the Telly but not really taking things in.

At 8.00 there was sign of movement in Moncur Drive. The girl had walked down the road and then across to the CT Club. Where she met her mate. David Jones had followed her in a minute or so later and then the Boss walked in to keep an eye on both parties. He quickly selected a seat where he could keep an eye on both of the parties.

The Boss was watching David Jones who was watching the two girls having a few drinks in the first set of seats when you walk in. David

Jones was sat in the second set of seats and half watching the Racing on the big screen TV. All the while he was keeping his eye on the two girls. The Boss was sat in the end row of seats and his problem was that there were too many locals who knew him and kept walking up to him asking for a game of snooker or pool. He fobbed them off by saying he was having a quiet drink alone as there was something going on at work he needed to think about. He was on Coke. It looks a bit like some of the darker beers and doesn't get you drunk. He had learned that in Auckland when he suddenly had a need to chase a villain and decided he was too drunk to do so. After that his DI reminded him to always go on coke when he is on tailing duty.it was something he had passed on to his juniors as well.

It must have been just after 10.00 pm when the girls decided to leave. The girl he was tailing had walked but the girl she had met was driving and she was not in a great condition. As usual the two girls had a big hug before they left. The Boss wondered why the hell girls did that even if they were going to see each other in the morning. He put it down as a girlie thing and concentrated on his task. so he walked carefully down the entrance to the CT club until it hit the road. He was perhaps 70 meters behind the guy he was tailing. The guy was around forty meters behind the girl. Another twenty meters and he would know if he was up for any excitement tonight. The girl turned to the left and the guy also turned to the left. The Boss quickened his step to keep up with the tailing. The girl had only about fifty meters before she turned to the right and into her driveway and he needed to make sure the guy was going the same way. He was hovering on the edge of going up her driveway so the Boss kept behind the fence of the entrance to the CT Club. The girl turned to the right and the guy, forty meters behind her also turned to the right as he walked up to her driveway. It looked like it was going to happen tonight!

The Boss hurried his pace so he could keep behind the guy he was tailing. He had to catch him in the act but not too far into the act that the woman was injured.

That's when he got on the phone to me. When I heard the phone I was in a half doze watching the TV. As always when I heard my phone go, I was instantly on full alert. Then I had to wonder where the hell I had left my phone. It was only a couple of meters away so I grabbed it and noticed the Boss was calling me. What could he want at this time?

The Boss was speaking in a quiet voice, "It looks like it is tonight. If you want to be a part of this, get on up here". Then the Boss's voice changed. It sounded like he was drunk! "Nah, won a couple of games of pool then that Mark bloke had me in the final. "(pause) nah he well beat me. 5 games to 1. Good night, mate! Yeah I should be home in five minutes. Wassat? Yeah, put the kettle on if you don't fancy a beer. Yeah, See ya." With that the phone went dead. While I was looking at the phone it rang again.

Again it was the Boss." Sorry about that. When I walked up to her drive the other bird's car was parked. Looks like she might be staying the night. Our lad must have decided he wasn't a match for two girls, so he walked away. No, that's when I had to pretend I was pissed and have the talk. I said goodnight to him, but he just grunted and carried on walking out of the drive and turned left. I assume he's on his way home, so I'll follow the lad and make sure he goes home. But it looks like you and me are on for an early night. I'll see you in the morning. No make it 3.00. Afternoon it is and you'll be covering the bloke tomorrow night."

With that the Boss's phone went dead and I was left high and dry. I mean I was ready for action when the Boss first rang and then he did his drunk bit and now I have to calm down and go to sleep? Fat chance. Looks like I might be in for a late evening of TV.

Thursday

I got to bed sometime after 3.00am. I ended up watching an Italian game of soccer before deciding I'd had enough. I slept fairly well, and I was in at the Office by 2.30.

Tim had an all in brawl at the Palace tavern just after 10.00 the previous evening. He got the Squaddies involved and then started to take statements. It got messy and he asked whoever was on duty to take over for him. That of course was Alan Kirk so not a lot got done beyond the perfunctory taking of statements. Fortunately at mid-morning Derek and Dave had turned up and stepped in to take over the interrogations.

At 2.45 the Boss breezed in, and we had a chat about the previous evening.

He mentioned that if we were going to be out tailing someone we should be armed. We could not possibly know if the offender was armed so we should be too. He had been thinking about this since he had been involved in the armed offenders callout. Now he had decided to take some action to protect his lads. It wasn't something I looked forward to. If you like it was another responsibility knowing I was carrying a loaded weapon.

The Boss was nothing but thorough. Within a half hour I was down in the Armory getting set up with a pistol. I declined the opportunity to grab a bullet proof vest as I was not taking this being armed thing seriously. Also down in the Armory were Mike Jackson and the Boss walked in as I was leaving and feeling very self-conscious about walking around with a loaded weapon.

At a little before 5.00 I left the office and started to tail David Jones. He was waiting a little up the road from this girls work. The Boss had told me this girls name was Sue. He had heard the conversation between the two girls and worked out which one was Sue. David got on the same bus as Sue although he was a couple of rows behind. Sue seemed oblivious to the fact that she was being followed. As for me I followed the Bus until it stopped around the corner from Moncur

Drive. Sue got off and then David got off as well. He turned towards Springfield Road, which was a disappointment to me, but he turned around once Sue had turned into Moncur Drive.

So far so good, I thought to myself. The Boss had given me a few ideas on the best way of tailing a suspect, so I used them. I parked at the top of Moncur drive and kept my car behind a shrub so I could watch the suspect from the comfort of my car drivers seat. It quickly went dark, but I could still see him under the streetlight. I kept an eye on him for as long as I could before I dozed off. Perhaps he moved which caught my attention. Whatever it was he was not there where I had been watching him. I admit I did start to panic, and I could hear the Sarge saying, 'whatever you do, don't panic!' He had told me this when I first faced a gang of street thugs with him. His demeanor on that occasion saved the day as we faced off the street thugs with a lofty disdain. Today I remembered his words as I tried to take notice of my surroundings and then the suspect walked up the road towards me. A passerby had entered the street so David had turned and walked up the road until the passerby entered a house and then resumed his initial watching point.

He suddenly appeared in my eyeline as he walked up the street. Someone else had walked into the street so he had casually walked up the street. He walked right past my car without seeing me so I could still use the cover of the Shrubbery. He would have been there for over a couple of hours when Sue appeared as if she was going to the CT Club. She walked up the driveway to the club and went inside. I was a little late in noticing this development so when David walked into the Club after her I decided to drive down and park in the car park.

Around the corner Mike Jackson had followed his lad to the home of the girl he was following in Springfield Road. Mike was fifty meters up the road and had a good vantage point. After perhaps a half hour Mike had noticed his guy, Johnny Scarrow, had actually walked down the driveway to the girls front door and he was knocking on the door.

Mike edged quite close to the property and was adjacent to the next door property as he waited to see what developed. Mike was in that unfortunate position of not knowing whether to ring the Boss and or me to say things were developing. He was in a quandary because he was almost convinced he was now tailing the Murder suspect, but he did not want to pull me off the guy I was tailing, just in case. He rang the Boss who told him to try and creep up to the window and see if he could hear what Johnny Scarrow was up to. Mike did the best that he could and heard reasonable discussion that did not appear too heated. He retreated and rang the Boss again but could not get the Boss to pick up his cellphone.

He acted on his own decision and walked up to the door and knocked on the door.

Sue was sat in the same seat she had occupied last night. David was a row or two over and it gave me a chance to sit and observe them both. Using the Boss's technique I was on straight Coke, and it looked like Monteiths Dark ale which they served in the Club. I couldn't make out what David was drinking but he was drinking it very slowly. Sue had met a different mate in the club, and they were gossiping away like a couple of old friends. I have to say that this Sue was quite a good looking young girl. I'd reckon she worked out occasionally, but she was certainly a nice looker, and she was dressed to the nines although she might have been said to have been dressed a little provocatively. She was showing the goods, as they were. Not overly provocative but well dressed in a modern sort of way. Sue was not being overly careful with her drinking. There at least a few occasions when I reckon someone could have roofied her drink if they were that way inclined. David never went near her, so I was satisfied on the score.

It was probably just before ten that sue, and her mate got up and left the club. David was a few feet behind them and walked as if he was going to his car in the car park. He turned to the right and Sue and her mate went to the left. Sue's mate got in her car halfway down the hill and Sue carried on home. David had immediately backpedaled on turning right and was following Sue at a distance down the driveway. I was fifty meters behind David and being as stealthy as I could. I watched David follow Sue from behind the Punga trees at the entrance of the CT club. It occurred to me I was doing exactly the same as the Boss had done the previous night. I hoped I would not be in the same position as the Boss and have to pretend I was drunk again. David followed Sue up her right of way and I followed David and watched him from the end of the right of way.

It was one of those clear nights and I could hear Sue fumbling in her bag for her keys. As I was watching David looked poised and ready to leap on Sue when she opened her door. I was in something of a quandary. I wanted to get him in the act of attacking her, but I had to be careful in letting him attack her before I er... drew my weapon. It was really bugging me that I had a loaded firearm in my holster. And I had really no idea whether I drew the weapon before or after the arrest or whenever. My mind instantly started to wander. Obviously I should draw my weapon before I engaged David and that was when it all happened. David rushed out and overpowered Sue immediately she got the front door open. He had her inside and the front door was closed before I knew it. It all happened so fast I was momentarily stunned and in that brief opportunity I knew I had lost my best chance of apprehension.

I was moving forward and then I thought about ringing the Boss. I had my phone out and was ringing the boss before I was even aware of what I was doing. The Boss answered immediately "Hello" was his opening.

"Boss, He's inside and I didn't get in with him to stop him. Ideas! Please!"

"Shit! Knock on the door and tell him you're lost. Anything to distract him. That girl's life is at stake. I'm on my way."

I walked up to the door and knocked loudly. Inside there was quiet after I knocked. I knew there were at least a couple of people inside. I knocked again and I could hear him inside and moving to the front door. He roughly opened the door and said "Yes?"

I was thinking on my feet, so I said the first thing that came into my head. "Oh. yeah. Hi. Is Sue in?"

He was also thinking on his feet by his surprised response. "Er, no. I'm feeding her cats. Is there a message."

Again I am thinking on my feet. "She doesn't have a cat. You feeding her dog, then?"

He replied. "Yeah, It's her dog. Now if you have nothing else?" and he started to close the door.

I was at a loss, so I asked him. "So, when is she back then?" Please be aware I am not at my usual best when I get caught flatfooted, as it were.

"Er...Saturday?" and he closed the door in my face.

I knocked again. He was a little slower in opening the door. In my imagination I could hear the victims muffled voice in the background. I immediately thought he probably had tape over her mouth.

He opened the Door. "What!"

I said the first thing that I could think of. "I'm Mark. Can you tell her I called round to see her?"

He again slammed the door in my face. As far as I was concerned I had given the girl an extra few seconds. I went back to stand at the end of her drive, and I saw the Boss running up the driveway.

He was all business. "I'm going round the back. If you hear me kick the back door in, you kick the front door in. Gottit?"

With that he was gone around the side of the property.

I was waiting for the sound of a door being kicked in and I heard nothing. I was waiting by the front door. For those keeping count, I still had not drawn my weapon. Yes, I am well out of my depth in this situation.

I heard a noise out to the side of the carport and David was on the run. He had gone out of the door to the carport and was running quietly down the drive and then turning to his left to flee the right of way. I shouted 'Stop. Police and armed." Yes that is not the usual call out, but as I said, I am out of my depth in this situation. At this point I actually drew my pistol out of its shoulder holster.

I noticed another figure coming up the driveway.' Oh Great', I thought now we have a bloody Civilian involved. Do I holster the pistol, or do I fire? There is something you need to do. Oh Yeah. Make sure that beyond the target is clear of any possible shooting victim. The Guy coming up the driveway seemed to move to one side of the fleeing Suspect and then something wonderful happened. As he moved away he turned it into a move towards the suspect. He then had the suspect in a choke hold and within a few seconds the suspect was out on the ground.

By now I had caught up with the suspect and the passer by. I was about to thank the passerby for his efforts when I realised the passerby was Mike Jackson. The Boss had told him to come round to Moncur Drive immediately as we had a case going south. Now I had thought a bit more about it. Mike had used a clothesline hold on the suspect and then used a sleeper hold on him which was why he had gone out like a light. According to Mike he had used something that sounded like a 'Tagashi' on him. Evidently Mike was also a black belt in Tae Kwon Do. It's amazing that we didn't know about Mike's other passion for Tae Kwon do but it's something we don't find out about until we are tested.

Just then the Boss came running up to us and we all holstered our weapons and congratulated Mike on his takedown.

I was sent inside to see how the girl was. She was still terrified and still tied up with Duct tape. She knew how close to death she had come. Her mind was recalling everything she had read about the serial killer and she knew she was his next victim. When she heard noises coming from around the back she wondered what the heck was going on and then her assailant had gone running to the side door, she thought she may have a faint chance of surviving the ordeal. She could hear noises coming from outside her door and she did not know what was happening. Then I had forced open her front door and she knew then that she was saved. She couldn't get out her thanks quickly enough when I removed the tape from her mouth and I was the obvious recipient of her gratitude. For me, I felt terrible. I had put this girl in danger with my mind wandering at the crucial point, when she was pushed inside and the door was closed. No, I didn't feel like she should be thanking me.

I released her and rang for an ambulance to attend. They were there within a few minutes and then all of the chaos associated with an arrest ensued. We had a couple of squad cars blocking the road. We had the neighbours out on the street busy having a look see. Because the Squaddies had blocked the road there was one bloke arguing about how he needed to get home as his misses would be worrying. The Squaddie took everything in his stride and gave him a breathalyzer. He failed. He should have just kept his mouth shut.

The Ambulance arrived and the girl was fine if a little shook up. She had been letting herself into her front door when her world collapsed around her. She immediately thought about Rotorua's serial Killer and thought she was a goner. She then kept thanking the Boss who told her I was the hero, and she should thank me. The Boss just wanted to get on with booking this Murderer. Eventually when the ambulance had gone, and the Squaddies had taken the Murderer back to the station the Boss had a quiet word with me.

"I want you in my office at ten this morning." And that was it. He walked off to speak to Mike and I was left alone wondering if I had nearly got this girl killed.

I asked the Boss if I needed to go back to the station to book this bloke and he told me to go home and have a good night's rest.

I may have gone home but I did not have a good night's rest.

Chapter 12

The Judge had a bad night on the previous night. He had followed the girl up to the CT Club and the Girl was drinking with her friend. At the conclusion he had mentally prepared himself to decide on the girls fate. He had followed her back from the club and this girl she had been drinking with had already driven to the Girls house. She was either too drunk to drive or they had other means of entertainment available to the pair of them. Was this just another sin to have to deal with? He had to turn around and retreat from the girls house and leave her fate to another night. On his way out he had passed a man who cheerily shouted something, but this man was also drunk. He was probably going to a house in Kiwi Street. He was loudly speaking on his phone. Why do people think they need to speak louder when they are drunk? He had turned out of Moncur Drive and summoned a taxi to take him home. He had decided it was the girls fate that was in her hands. Perhaps he would ask her if the friend she had been drinking with had then engaged in lesbian activities. The Bible was silent on lesbian activity but was very strict on homosexual activity. Perhaps it was something he could ask the Minister about some day.

On Thursday he had decided to follow the girl home again. If she went to the CT Club he would know she was in the habit of regularly getting drunk and that would be just another black mark against her.

He was almost pleased when she got dressed again to go out to her local. If nothing else it would mean her reflexes would be a little slower when he pounced. He watched from his vantage point inside the club and then he followed her down the Driveway of the Club and followed her home. It was almost too easy to gain advantage of the girl when she was the worst for wear. Within a second or two he had secured her to a chair from her kitchen table and she was ready to be questioned. When the Front door of her property was knocked on, at first he told the girl to be quiet and kept quiet himself. If the people knocking on the door believed there was no one home, they would go away.

When the knocking was repeated he answered the door. Behind him he could hear the girl trying to shout something, even though he had a piece of tape across her mouth. He answered the Door, and it was quite probably a former boyfriend looking for easy sex. It was yet another black mark against the girl that she would have old boyfriends knocking on her door at all hours of the night. He answered the door and could not really remember what he said. He had the Blood rushing in his ears and he said something that shut off the man at the door's enquiry.

When he knocked on the door again the Judge was puzzled but it was only the same man asking to be remembered to the girl. Now at last he could get on with asking the girl if she was about to repent in her ways. He somehow knew she would not repent! He still had the tape across her mouth when he thought he heard a noise coming from the area around the back door. Evidently the caller at the front door was persistent and was now trying around the area of the back door. Was there no end to this old boyfriend looking for easy sex!

He made an instant decision that this girl had too many friends and he should leave. The man had knocked on the front door and now he was around the back of the house. He knew this house style and he also knew that it had a side door into the carport. He left the woman still tied up with Duct tape and he departed by the side door. He was exiting the carport when he heard a noise from the front door. Surely the friend had not come to the front door again. He ran off down the driveway and that was the last thing he remembered until he woke up in the Cells.

Friday

I was in at 9.00 ish and I had a coffee with the sarge. I couldn't really tell him I might get fired for cocking up a Murder investigation.

Somehow the Sarge already had an idea that something was up, but he didn't say anything and neither did I.

It seems that the previous evening Mike Jackson had followed the girl and Johnny Scarrow to Springfield Road. When Johhny had knocked on the door, Mike had crept forward and rang the Boss. Taking note of the Boss's suggestion he had gone to the window and could only hear what he thought was polite conversation. When he had tried the Boss again he didn't get a reply, so he acted on his own initiative. He knocked on the door and had his Police ID held behind his back. The girl had answered the door, so Mike showed her his Police ID. She was very grateful to See Mike and mouthed silently, 'There's some guy in my house. Do Something."

That was all Mike needed. He drew his gun and motioned for the girl to step back into the Kitchen. He went into the lounge and arrested the guy. He would worry about what charges later on. Once he had the area secure he called a Squad car who took Johnny Scarrow down to the Station. Mike gave the girl a lift, in his car, to the station. She agreed to press charges, so Mike got his suspect for stalking charges and that was just for a starter. The girl agreed to press charges and Mike was still tying up the paperwork when he got a call from the Boss telling him to get round to Moncur Drive 'Sharpish'.

I hung around for a half hour and the Boss noticed I was in early, so he called me in to his office.

I hung my head a little sheepishly. I knew I was in for a bollocking and possibly even for the sack. I had cocked up a murder investigation and had even place the life of a young girl in danger. I wondered if the Boss could sack me or whether it would have to be done by the Big Boss. I rather hoped that if it came to a sacking the Boss would do it. The Big Boss would take too much happiness from seeing me go.

The Boss opened with. "You really cocked up last night and you endangered a girl's life. What the hell happened?"

I mumbled something about being so overcome with having a weapon that I had allowed my attention to wander and missed my opportunity.

He asked me to speak clearly and then said that whatever was said within his office would stay in the office.

I told him again about my thinking sideways at the moment I should have attacked the suspect.

He said. "That's it?"

"Yep". I knew if I was unable to stand with a firearm I was out.

He said something which rather surprised me. "So you reckon it's my fault for not having you good with guns and stuff."

"No Boss. It's me. I'm just not good with guns. Maybe I haven't had that much training."

"Yeah, that sounds like it's still my fault. Hang on."

He got on the phone to somewhere and had a conversation with someone. When he got off the phone he said. "Right, all sorted. You go to Trentham on the 9th of next month for the AOS training course. It's a four day course and at the end of it you will be comfortable with any firearm. Starting next month you will be running a monthly firearms familiarization course for the CIB. Everyone who wants to use a firearm has to be vetted by you. Any other issues you have? Good. I thought you were going to resign today. Glad to see it was really my fault. Right shall we go and see our murder lad now? See if we can get him to admit to the other three murders and that girl he let off."

I was a bit shaken that the Boss had taken my doubts and saw it as a fault with his leadership. I could see it from both sides, and he may have a point, but I will always see it as initially my problem that I could not voice my concerns to him or even the Sarge.

The Boss was already walking down to the cells, and I had to hurry to catch up with him.

The suspect was already up for kidnapping the girl from last night. That was at least what we had on him. He refused to speak to us.

Reckoned he had a mission to perform, and it was a higher calling that we would not understand.

I had the idea that we should get the Minister from his church in to have a word with him. After we had explained to the Minister what had been going on he was more than happy to speak with David.

David and the minister spoke for a good half hour and Pete the Minister walked out and reckoned he would admit to last night's offence but after that we had a problem.

We told Pete about him visiting with whores and casting his seed on the belly etc. Pete went back in to try again thinking he could use one of his sermons to counter Davids argument, but he met with little success. We thanked him for trying and said we would keep in touch.

I ducked home at lunchtime. Something told me I should, and when I checked my mailbox the parcel I had ordered was there. I was very careful lifting it out of the mailbox and into an evidence bag. That afternoon we got the prints lifted and we had a match for the prints left at the previous weeks murder.

When we approached David he was reluctant to tell us anything but once he knew we had him for the murder last week he confessed to all of the murders and also to the girl who repented and he let off.

The Boss was delighted and so was everyone else on the team. Even Alan Kirk was delighted we had someone in custody.

The Sarge reckoned we should all go out for a beer that night. He organised it and we started at the Belgian bar. Where we ended up I do not remember but it was a good night and something we all deserved after getting so much grief from the Big Boss. Even Alan Kirk joined us. He looked a bit the worse for wear when we poured him into a taxi as he had to cover the office the next day.

Right. I usually say how the Crims went.

David Jones got 25 years to life which effectively meant 25 years. He reckoned he would be a beacon inside for those who sought the light. I reckoned he might be a beacon but not in the way he was thinking of.

We never heard any more from Shi Low and his associates beyond our usual monthly cup of Tea. Also we never had any more armed robberies from Dairies.

Oh Yes. Our rapist appeared again. Not the religious guy, the other one. He grabbed an underage girl who had been in the pub and drinking. He took her down a side street off the top of Old quarry road. He did the deed and we had the issue of getting her to talk as she had been drinking in the pub. We had to convince her about not charging her with drinking before she would say anything about the rape. Maybe I'll leave that to the next book, if there is a next one.

What else happened? I went to Trentham and did my course. Provided I remembered that the weapon was my lifeline and I respected it, it would always respect me. When I got back to the Rotorua Station I did implement a training group for our CIB lads, and they all passed which I took as a feather in my cap. We also got into a monthly routine of marksmanship on the target range. The sarge got involved and he was a very good marksman. I think he won the monthly shootout probably five times out of the following year. The Key thing for me that whenever we went on a call where firearms were involved I was the accepted leader and I called the shots, as it were. As a feather in my cap I was also called out twice to take charge of the AOS on a callout when the leader was out of town.

During the course of the next few months I also sat and took my Senior sergeants Exam. I passed the exam, but it was a much tougher exam than I expected. My Boss encouraged me to consider taking my BA in Criminology. He already had his, but he had passed it twenty years ago. Did I want to sit through another five years of papers? The Boss worked on me as being his replacement when he retired, and he was probably going to take an early retirement. He reckoned he might have a nice little nest egg by then. I did sign up for the course but because I have to keep renewing my grant application through the force I could at least decide every year whether I wanted to do the next year.

On the Sunday we had our golf game with the Big Boss. The Sarge and I won by a couple of Stapleford points and the Big Boss again had to go to a Lodge meeting. We shook hands and the three of us went up to the bar for a beer which the Boss was happy to pay for. Hopefully we would not have another game with the Big Boss anytime soon which would mean he would have to play with me as his partner and I wouldn't wish that on anyone!

Alan Kirk had a couple of more weeks with us before he was seconded back to the Squaddies again. Dave Powell was transferred to Invercargill and received a swap for him in the guise of Bernie McDowell. My only problem was that Bernie McDowell was a girl officer. Her real name was Bernardette McDowell! Again, she was a Senior constable on transfer, but we know had to tone down our language when she was around. Other than that she was a very capable officer.

The Boss got a call from the Big Boss on the Friday we arrested the Murderer, and he walked up to the Big Boss's office with a grin on his face. He did mention about the Shi Low and my cuppa with him but the Big Boss wisely decided we had nothing to go on so we should keep it as an open case.

Johnny Scarrow got a good behaviour bond for stalking the girl, so he was found guilty and he did have a criminal record of sorts. Pete, the Minister was involved with Johnny's rehab, and I think that between them they sorted Johnny Scarrows love life out. He was involved in a steady relationship the last time I talked to Pete.

The week after the game with the Big Boss the three mates were having their weekly game at Springfield, Colin and Dave and Mark. Mark was one shot up on Colin and two shots up on Dave. As always teeing off on the tenth Mark had gone for a bull blooded swing to get over the 'halfway hill' and ended up in the middle of the eighth fairway.

When Mark walked off to play his recovery from the Eighth fairway Colin and Dave were having their usual chat.

"So what do you reckon that Ronnie should do". Asked Colin.

"That depends on his numbers. If he has managed to recruit a few good lads he should probably have a go against 'Tohi'. You still reckon there's not a good chance of getting some of Tohi's take then he should have a go at wiping the rivals out. If you reckon we can get a cut from Tohi's action then we should play one off against the other. Either way it will be seen as a gang war so there's no downside for us, the thin blue line in the middle". Replied Dave.

"What do you reckon about that Johnny Scarrow lad?" asked Colin.

"I reckon he will reoffend. He's that type." Replied Dave.

"Is it time to get the Panel back up and running?"

"It's probably overdue. Have you found a fixer yet?" asked Dave.

"Yeah. There's a guy in Taupo that looks like a starter. I've had a chat with him, and he sounds like he could be good for us."

"Well I have three lads in the Lodge. What do you reckon we give it a test run?"

"I reckon that Johnny Scarrow could be a starter. Just a beating for the first one. Let him know we don't tolerate that behaviour in town. Hang on, here comes Mark. Did you see where his second shot went?"

"In the trees on the edge of the tenth. He'll be lucky to get a six or a seven." Replied Dave.

"Hey Mark, for the back nine do you fancy going off the ladies tee. The way you are playing I reckon the girls wouldn't mind." Shouted Colin.

And that is where we shall leave the three mates, just having a good natured game of golf.

Other work by the same Author

Soul Purpose

Vol 1 & 11 & 111

A fiction work with something of a twist

He has returned.

The subtitle is "and it's so not what you think" Probably one of the most fun books I have written and probably the most amusing. The Son of God has returned, and he finds the world is in something of a state. Partly because of what he said and did a couple of thousand years ago on his last visit here. Yeah, it's all a bit confused now he is back. Let's see how he deals with it!

Mickey Carter: An angel with L-plates

It's funny and set in South Manchester. It's easy being an angel. Isn't it?

I have Angels at my table.

An interesting story set in England as natural disasters occur and somehow the higher levels of heaven are involved.

Danny Casanova's legacy

A fun story centred around a young guys first venture into the world of grown ups and doing what grown ups do. Or at least trying to!

Time and time again.

A book about past life experiences. Interestingly it only deals with past lives on planet earth.

Police series

A series about crime in 'Rotorua'

Book1 The Panel

Book 2 The Party

Book 3 The Judge

Book 4 The War

Boof 5 The payoff.

About the Author

Andy has been writing for the last twenty years and has written a number of books over a wide variety of genre. His first book Sold over 5000 copies and he continues to write on whatever the mood takes him. Currently he is finishing Books on the crime scene in Rotorua, New Zealand. As always his books are not meant to be taken seriously. If you haven't laughed today, read one of Andy's books!

Printed by Libri Plureos GmbH in Hamburg, Germany